Eelgrass

Tori Curtis

COOPERSTOWN, NEW YORK

Tori Curtis
14 Walnut St
Cooperstown, NY 13326
www.toricurtiswrites.com

Book Layout ©2013 BookDesignTemplates.com

Epigraph is "Eel-Grass" by Edna St. Vincent Millay, first published in *Second April*, 1921.

Eelgrass/ Tori Curtis. -- 1st ed.
ISBN 978-1-945548-01-7

for those of us who were there

No matter what I say,
All that I really love
Is the rain that flattens on the bay,
And the eel-grass in the cove;
The jingle-shells that lie and bleach
At the tide-line, and the trace
Of higher tides along the beach:
Nothing in this place.

—EDNA ST VINCENT MILLAY

"HAVE YOU TALKED TO YOUR BROTHER TODAY?"
BETTAN ASKED. It was early afternoon and they
were sprawled on the rocks, warming themselves
in the sun.

"Rees? No, why?" Efa stretched her arms above her head
and yawned. She and her brother were close, but they lived
apart now that they were both grown. Sometimes they could
go days without speaking.

"I saw him this morning. He said another ship docked in
town late last night." Village life was quiet, so they often had
to find their amusement in the local humans' affairs. But this
wasn't much news - ships came into harbor all the time.

"Did it?" she said.

"A big one."

Efa rolled over onto her side so she could see Bettan,
mindful of the sharp rocks under her hip. Bettan was wearing
a little ragged wisp of a cotton dress, suitable for around the
selkie village (where nudity was an occasional fact of life) but
not enough to take into town. And she was smiling hopefully,

looking up through her eyelashes. Efa said, "I'm sure I've never seen anything so grand as this boat," and let the final word drop.

"It's not just a boat," Bettan corrected. Then she charged ahead like she had expected and planned against the possibility of a lukewarm reception. "Besides, you know all the men will be looking for a good time."

Efa groaned. "I don't even like sailors."

Bettan liked sailors. She liked their thick, corded arms and the exotic stories they had for any girl who would sit by them. And then - well, then there was Bettan herself. She had soft inky hair to her waist, a pair of little elegant hands that were as at home in a pair of white lace gloves as they were shucking oysters. She had a way of looking at a person like they were the most precious thing in the world. Bettan liked sailors, and the sailors liked her right back.

"It's not just that," Bettan said, although it was her favorite part. "They'll be selling things, too - maybe something exciting!"

Efa hid her smile behind her hand. "We can never afford the exciting things," she said, but it was a weak protest.

"The fun's in seeing them, though." She sobered up a little, her smile gone serious. "Please swim over with me? We haven't done anything in days, I'm dying."

"Okay, fine. As long as I don't have to dance."

"Just with me," she promised, and Efa sighed.

The walk back to the village was a long one. They had to go quite a ways out if they wanted to avoid being spotted and, worse, given an assignment. As a child, Efa had loved living in the selkie village. There had always been other children to play with, people to teach her to hunt in seal form and out, adults to make sure that she was fed and clothed. Now that she was grown, old enough to have a husband and pups of her own but not yet in possession of either, the closeness of her home had become cloying. No one seemed sure what to do with her or what to think of her, except that she was too old to take care of and too young to contribute much.

Efa supposed she had gotten off easy, all things considered. The adults seemed to think she was good enough. She was strong and patient, perfectly happy to run errands or find food for people with busier lives. She liked to cook as much as a selkie needed to, and she could sew well enough that she often took in other people's mending. She had never been especially interested in boys and all their associated fuss, but even she expected that soon that would change and she would be a married woman. Bettan hadn't been so lucky. She was older, Rees's yearmate, and had never lost her lust for adventure.

Either way, they both avoided the village these days unless they had something to do or someone to meet. It was too easy for any of the real grown-ups to find a project for them.

"Do you think Rees is going to start trading with the humans?" Bettan asked quietly, stepping over a rock bigger than her head. They were walking through the water, sand squishing between their toes. They always went barefoot; it was one of the ways the humans in town could tell who was which. "He says if we get enough money together, get something they want, we'll have real bargaining power."

"What are you talking about?" Efa said. "He's twenty-four."

"That's not too young to accomplish something."

She tried to imagine her brother, all big shoulders and goofy smile, responsible for leading their people into a golden age of prosperity. In a decade, maybe, once he'd had a chance to settle out and try some of his ideas. "Yeah, like raising kids, maybe. Things people do normally." She ran a hand through her hair, fluffing it out. "This is all hypothetical, right?"

Bettan shrugged. "I heard some people talking. I don't know if they were serious."

"You heard him talking, is what you heard," Efa said, giggling, "about how he'd be king of the world soon."

Bettan laughed, too, but she was shaking her head. "You know your brother's not power-hungry."

Efa made a face. He wasn't at all. That was the problem. He was upstanding and brilliant. People liked her well enough, but they respected him. "Ugh, you're right," she said. "Even if they asked him to, he'd just be like 'What an honor!'"

"'Of course I'll serve my community however I can!'" Bettan said, striking a pose. They both smiled.

The village wouldn't have been easily recognized by a human as civilization. Most of their people, given the choice between wearing their sealskins or going out as humans, opted to live as seals. Human bodies were a hassle. They liked to be clothed. They were more susceptible to the elements. They couldn't dive as deep or hold their breath as long, and if they were tossed about under the waves, they came up sputtering and gasping for air. They couldn't catch fish as well, and were more finicky about eating it whole and raw. There was only one advantage Efa could see to shedding her sealskin, though it was a big one - the humans would, almost, accept her as one of them.

Their village looked out over the beach. There were no streets or churches, and any shops were run out of people's homes. The buildings were small and hunched over at awkward angles, like people looking for an excuse to leave a bad party. Selkies were no great builders, and rarely had the money or the inclination to pay for their houses. They had raised their village from the ground as a community effort, and it stayed standing by pure luck.

The houses Efa and Bettan walked to were off to the side, smaller and even more hunched than the others. They were each shared by four or five of the younger selkies, who generally didn't care much about privacy. Once they were married, they might move off into their own homes, but for now their stashes were so small there was nothing for their fellows to pick over.

Their houses were next door to each other. They waved and each went off into their own. Efa's had one square room, with a bed in the corner that could be used by anyone but rarely was. Along the wall she had a wooden crate that held everything she owned. A few dresses, a beaded bracelet that was a gift from her mother, her mending, some coins. A bag big enough to hold anything she might need to carry to town, plain but carefully oiled and waxed to keep water out. And on top of all that, folded reverently, was her most precious possession - her sealskin.

She lifted it out of the box and it slid into her arms. It was warm to the touch and friendly with her skin. It wanted to wrap itself around her. She hugged it to her chest for a moment and then started grabbing supplies. She selected a pale green gown, not her nicest but fancy enough for a night on the town, and stuffed it into her bag with some money. Then she pulled the dress she was wearing over her head and off, replacing it carefully in her crate.

When she got back outside, Bettan was waiting for her. She was undressed, too, and held a deep blue dress and a small money pouch in her hands. "I thought I'd borrow your bag this time," she said.

"You always borrow my bag," Efa said, but she held it out so Bettan could put her things in.

"It's better than mine."

They waited to change into their sealskins until they were down at the beach and knee-deep in water. Then they pulled them out and carefully stepped in, toes first. The change wasn't painful, even with all of the bones changing shape and organs reforming, but it was a little uncomfortable, like trying not to scratch an itchy spot. It took a particular sort of not paying attention to get it right. She fell to the water as a seal and, taking the straps of her bag in her mouth, they were off.

The beach near the human town was long and sandy, unlike the harsh, rocky shores of the island where the selkies lived. Efa and Bettan shed their sealskins and walked up out of the water, watching for other people. This stretch of beach was usually deserted. There were other bits of shoreline that were closer to town, and others still that were nicer. All this one had going for it was that it was relatively close to town, and a straight shot from the selkie island, so it had mostly been given up to their use.

They saw no one, so they kept going. Efa opened her bag and sighed.

"Is everything okay?" Bettan asked.

"Yeah," she said. "Water got in, is all."

She took out the dark blue dress, now dripping wet, and handed it to Bettan, who made a face and started to wring it out. "Just once," she murmured, "I'd like to own something that wasn't salt-stained."

"Don't be silly," Efa said. They couldn't afford clothes that wouldn't survive rough handling. They weren't like some of the more well-off town girls; they spent their time where it was wet and rocky.

They squeezed as much water as they could manage out of their dresses and put them on, then searched for a place to hide their sealskins. They couldn't just carry them into town

- they were too big - but they couldn't leave them out in the open, either. Any human who took possession of a selkie's sealskin had that selkie under their power. The selkie would be trapped, maybe forever.

Efa didn't want to worry about that, but she was careful. They chose a spot at the top of a hill where the grass grew in sandy patches and dug, with their bare hands, two holes for their sealskins. Once they were covered up, they each found three rocks and placed them in triangles on top of the skins to hold them down.

"Okay," Bettan said when they were done, "let's go, it's going to be dark soon."

They came into town with plenty of daylight left and got quickly to the job of sightseeing. The ship was indeed large, and even Efa had to admit that it was grand to behold. Even better, at least to Bettan's mind, the ship's master was selling rich fabric in such bright colors that they had never before seen them committed to cloth. Bettan spent altogether too much money on a bolt of luxurious scarlet that barely fit in Efa's bag, and spent half an hour thereafter stroking it.

"Promise me you'll make me a dress with it?" she said over and over again.

Efa wanted to disapprove, but she couldn't. It would be beautiful on her. It was exactly the color to make her look wild and dangerous. And it wasn't like they had anything else to spend money on.

Once the sun started to go down, they finished up their shopping and headed to the Hungry Hogfish. It was the largest and most reputable of the local inns. While it only had a few rooms on the second floor, the downstairs was warm and cheerful, and spacious enough to hold half the town. George, the owner, was perched behind the bar, and he waved to the girls as they came in. "Bettan, you made it!" he said, grinning. Then he looked behind her and nodded. "Efa."

George was a man coming into his fifties with a body like a barrel. He'd had three wives, all named Mary, the first two of whom had died suddenly and young. Local rumor said that the Hogfish had slurped their souls from their bodies; the work required to run it had been just too much. So far Mary III, who was maybe ten years older than Efa and Bettan, seemed to be made of hardier stuff. She had a baby strapped to her back and a rag in her hands, and was rubbing down the tables vigorously.

Bettan glanced over the room and smiled. Most of the tables were occupied by locals, fishermen and townspeople Efa recognized by sight if not by name, but the men clustered at the big tables in the center of the room were new. And happy to be there: they were all laughing a little too loudly and gulping Mary's good but perfectly ordinary fish stew with enthusiasm.

They didn't seem to notice as Bettan and Efa stepped up to the bar. Good - sometimes sailors came into town who were too interested. Those types would lick their lips like hungry beasts, their heads spinning around to watch the girls.

Things rarely got nasty, but those men required a lot of caution and stepping out of the way of groping hands. Luckily, (and the only reason Efa would put up with Bettan's man-hunting,) George always took their side if it came to a fight. He swore it was good business, that none of the local fishermen would look on him well if their sisters and wives couldn't stop by for a bowl of stew and some talk, and it was probably true. Certainly it cemented the Hogfish's reputation that someone could leave their young daughter there for an hour and return to find her no worse for the wear.

"I know it's been forever," Bettan said, leaning in, her hair falling across her face, "but I heard there was a ship in town, so I thought, why not visit?"

George smiled indulgently. Sometimes Efa thought it was a shame that Bettan was closer to him than to her own father, but of the two men, George did the better job looking out for her. "Did they have anything you liked?"

"Yes!" she said, and jumped for Efa's bag so she could take out her cloth.

While she was showing it off, Efa gathered enough coins to feed them both. "How's your family?" she asked.

"Good, good," George said. "Can you believe it, my oldest boy's looking to get married."

Efa blinked. He was older than they were, but not by much. "That's great. Soon?"

"We're thinking next month."

"The question is, do you like the bride?" Bettan said.

George shrugged. "When it's your family, no one's ever really going to be good enough," he hedged, "but she seems like a nice girl."

"Then we're happy for you," Efa said. If she wasn't careful, Bettan could drag them into a conversation that would last for days. "Could we get something to eat and drink, please?"

She handed over the coins. George gave a cursory inspection and pocketed them. "Mary!" he called. "These girls need you to take care of them."

They walked to the middle of the room and took a table next to the sailors. Mary brought them each a bowl of stew, a mug of beer, and a small loaf of the coarse dark bread she made. Efa was starving. She started immediately on the stew, which was rich and thick with clams. Bettan sipped her beer, smoothed her dress, looked out of the corners of her eyes at the men around them.

"You're going to scare them if you keep on like that," Efa said.

"I'm sure they're brave." Bettan said it like the idea appealed.

"Me, too, but you can be intimidating."

Bettan rolled her eyes, but settled in her seat. She even broke off a piece of bread and dipped it in her stew.

And then, sure enough, one of the sailor boys turned to her. He was handsome, with mussed hair, warm brown skin and a charming smile. Efa wanted to like him. Then he said, "No one told me the girls were so pretty here," and she had to stop herself from laughing.

"I told you," said one of his friends, a grisly fellow with a wind-chapped face. "You spend enough time at sea and any old hag'll be easy on your eyes."

Bettan gasped at the insult, and the game began. The boys fell over themselves to assure her that she was the loveliest thing they'd ever seen. She looked at them with coy eyes and laid her delicate hands on their biceps. Efa savored the big chunks of fish in her stew and gulped her beer with relish. Before she knew what was happening they'd shoved their tables together and were three verses into a bawdy drinking song. Bettan had that effect on people.

By the time Efa finished her food (and the rest of Bettan's - she was too busy making friends to focus on it) they had convinced the Hogfish's fiddler to play a jaunty tune, and Bettan was doing her level best to dance with everyone. Efa watched them from over the rim of her mug. This was all tradition by now. Bettan got to flirt, and Efa got to make fun of her afterwards. That way they were both happy.

An old man's drink thudded hard on the table next to her.

Efa looked up and was relieved to discover that he wasn't interested in her in particular. He was just languid, feeling all right, having a good time with his pals. From the stench of him she suspected he'd brought his own something to imbibe in between sips of beer. "But the most beautiful girl I ever saw-" he started.

("Not this one again," said one of the younger men.)

"-was a vicious she-wyrm from the darkest depths!"

Efa couldn't help herself. "A serpent?"

"Eh," said one of the others. "He gets a little poetic when he's, you know."

"We try not to encourage him," agreed a third.

But she was fascinated. She leaned in, and she could see the strands of his beard like a boar's hair brush.

"She was a fishwife," he said. "A fine woman, stark naked in the water, and then, right here," he tapped his hipbone, "where things start to get interesting, poof! A fish!"

Down the table, a scrawny youth jeered, and Efa barely heard his words. "I'd bet you can still find something interesting to do with one of those. She's still got-"

"I didn't know fishwives were real," she said, barely able to form the words over her blush. People told stories about them, but then, people told stories about kings, too. She'd never known anyone who'd met one.

"As real as you are," he said, and pinched her arm playfully. "I was near sixteen, just a lad, been to sea no more than a year. One night there was this dreadful storm, and as it let up I saw her by moonlight."

"I thought they travelled in schools," Efa said, "like fish."

"Ah!" he said, and his eyes were wide and bloodshot, those of a man who had lived long enough to gray without a woman to look after him. "But not all fish hide beneath the others. Imagine a fish the likes of which your fishermen would die to catch, a fish that rules all else."

She nodded.

"Now think of the fish who lives to eat that fish. That's a fishwife, my girl."

"When they group together, they sink ships, don't they?" Bettan asked, startling Efa. The music had stopped; she was back at the table, a man's arm around her waist.

Efa had heard those stories before. She wasn't surprised by the murmurs of agreement around the table. "But how?" she asked. "They're just fish-people. They don't have-"

"What does it matter, how?" Bettan said, merry. "They destroy. It's in their nature."

"They ensnare you," the sailor said, quick to turn the subject back to himself. "I stood on deck and watched her, and she stared back with these black eyes, as dark as the places a drowned man sinks - eyes like yours." He pointed at Bettan, though by their eyes Efa and Bettan were indistinguishable. "And then she began to sing."

"A love song?" Efa asked.

He shook his head. "Next thing I remember, I was in the water, in the wyrm's embrace. She was soft like a woman, but sharp like a knife, and she tore the clothes from my body." The men were all hooting and elbowing each other. Bettan raised one eyebrow and they straightened up, brushed off their shirts. The old sailor coughed uncomfortably. "I'm sorry, you girls don't need-"

Bettan leaned forward and looked up through her lashes at him. "We're old enough for practically anything," she said. "And Efa wants to hear your story."

He looked torn, but after a moment he went on. "The witch nearly drowned this poor soul," he said.

"What stopped her?" Efa said.

One of the sailors up the table gave a short, handsome laugh. "She was only looking for a little bit of man," he explained, "to get her through the night."

Efa didn't think that was the sort of thing a person should say, especially not to a girl he'd just met, but Bettan was delighted. "It must be awfully lonely for them, all alone in the deep dark sea." She traced the curve of her lower lip with her pointer finger. "I know a little bit about that."

Efa jumped up and reached across the table to give Bettan a shove. "You go," she said. "Go dance some more. You are unbelievable."

Bettan stood primly and returned to the makeshift dance floor, along with half a dozen of the sailors. She winked over a man's shoulder and Efa sighed. She tapped her feet to the fiddle and asked for more ale and by the time she looked up (maybe she deserved it, wishing for a night with a friend who was more like her) Bettan was gone.

At first she assumed that Bettan had left with one of the sailors, but they were all accounted for. And they all had the same story: she had been happily dancing and making conversation, and then she'd excused herself and headed right out the door. George said he'd thought she just needed a breather.

Efa didn't believe it, but she said her goodbyes calmly and tried not to get angry. Once or twice before Bettan had gone off without her to do something exciting. It wasn't completely unexpected. But that had been when they were still girls, and she'd promised not to ditch her like that again.

Sometimes people were surprised that constant, dull Efa was best friends with a girl who lived for shiny baubles and was always getting into trouble. Mostly Efa didn't care. She knew she was so much more interesting when she was with Bettan, and Bettan was a better person when she was with her. People could talk all they wanted.

She just hated it when they were proven right.

It was pouring rain outside. Efa double-checked that her bag was sealed and Bettan's fabric safe within it. There was no way anyone would come out into this weather for a breath of fresh air. It wasn't windy or exhilarating like a good thunderstorm, just cold and dreary, and so thick it was impossible to see more than a few buildings away. Whatever George and the sailors thought, Efa knew better. Bettan would never have traded the warmth and excitement of the Hogfish for this.

She walked down the streets, too embarrassed to call out for Bettan but determined that she had to search. Maybe she had gone to spend the evening with one of her friends in town, and she would soon realize that she'd left without a word. Efa could already picture the apology, the way she'd hang her head and tell stupid jokes and say she was such an idiot, could she ever be forgiven? And Efa would be mad as ever but she'd forgive her, helplessly, the way she always did.

She had herself almost convinced that it would go that way as she left town. The woods leading to the beach were quiet and eerie at night. Efa was used to walking through with company, a friend or a brother to remind her that she was the most supernatural thing around for ages. She wrapped her arms around her chest to ward off the cold.

She got to her sealskin quickly and joyfully - she was freezing, and her seal body was much better suited for nasty weather. She had marked it with three big gray rocks scattered in a wide triangle. She always picked boring rocks to keep her sealskin from floating away if the wind picked up and blew away the sand covering it. Bettan was the one who looked specifically for the sparkly rocks, and set them so their most appealing sides were visible.

Efa looked over to make sure Bettan's sealskin was okay, and frowned. There was a hole where it had been buried.

She covered her open mouth with a hand and looked around, suddenly scared that someone might still be there. Bettan wouldn't have left without telling her, just to go home. More damning, she wouldn't have left a gaping hole in the beach. They always smoothed the sand over afterwards so no one would be able to tell where they hid their sealskins. They'd been living with the fear of theft their whole lives, they were careful about these things.

She fell to her knees and started digging for her skin. She was sure that it was there, except that suddenly she wasn't, and needed proof. The sand was gritty and rough from the rain, but she'd done this so many times before that she hardly noticed. Her fingers touched her sealskin. She pulled it up and into her lap, her breathing slowing as she brushed the sand off of it. It was sleek and damp, and it was still hers.

She found her brother on the other side of the selkies' island, on a shore he went to sometimes when he wanted to be alone. He wanted to be alone fairly often. They were both friendly, but while Efa would seek out other selkies even while she did her mending, Rees believed in spending a good chunk of time each day with no one but his thoughts.

She ignored her guilt at interrupting him and clambered out of the surf. He was stretched out on the sand, trees above shielding him from the rain. Rees's body was longer and wider than hers, even though she had reached her full growth. (She was still jealous.) When he shed his sealskin, he had big hands and scruff on his chin.

"It's awfully late," he said in Sealish while she was still occupied with the ungainly work of finding a comfortable place to sit.

"You're still up," she said.

"I could be trying to sleep."

Efa wiggled uncomfortably. She had wasted more than an hour getting back home and finding Rees, and she still had no idea what was going on. Her suspicions were enough to make her sick with nerves. "I think something awful just happened," she said.

She felt his attention shift, and relaxed. He'd always been this way when they were younger, too. So focused and calm. "What happened?" he said. "Are you okay?"

"I'm fine," she said. "It's - I think someone stole Bettan's sealskin."

He was quiet for a moment, and it occurred to her that this was much bigger than anything she'd brought to him as a child. "Are you sure? She'd probably be off with them by now."

"We were in town," she said, "and she just left for no reason. And her skin's missing."

"Hey now," he said, warm, "that might just be Bettan. She's always been hard to pin down."

"But we were at the Hogfish. She was dancing."

Everyone knew Bettan would dance all night if she could, and through most of the morning. Rees conceded the point with a sigh. "Even if you're right, this might not be a bad thing. No one's going to hurt her." If she'd been a man, there would have been the fear that she'd been taken so she could do hard labor. Selkies were strong, and there was no harder worker than a selkie man whose skin had been taken from him. But she was a beautiful young woman, so there was only one good reason why anyone would want her.

Efa shuddered all the way down to her hind flippers. "She'd make a miserable wife, you know she would."

"She's got to settle down eventually. You're old enough you should be, and she's my age."

"No one's making you get married," she pointed out, but she sounded small.

"That's different," he said, and something about the way he said it made her believe him. "I'm trying to figure myself out, I don't have time for a family yet. But Bettan, she needs something to do. A husband would be perfect for her."

It had to be true. It was what everyone said. The idea still made her sick. "One of us, though. She wouldn't marry a human if she got a choice." He just looked at her, and she stopped, embarrassed. If she was honest, Bettan was more intrigued by humans than anyone else she knew. They always joked that some day she would wed a ship's captain and see the world. Efa had hoped it would stay a joke.

Rees took pity on her. "Do you have any idea who did it?" he asked. "We could go to visit them, and then you'll see that she's just fine."

"It could have been anyone. Half the town is in love with her."

He made soft, soothing noises. She tried to rein herself in, not to be so obviously upset. "I'm sure she'll turn up."

Efa wasn't so sure. And if she did, it might be too late. "I want to tell everyone, so they all know they have to help me get her back."

"You can't do that," he said. "You shouldn't bother them with something this ridiculous."

She hadn't expected him to just go along with it. Their village survived mostly because everyone had quietly agreed to get along and not bother each other. But she hadn't expected to be so thoroughly shot down, either. "It's not. Someone kidnapped her and you think I'm ridiculous?"

Efa knew she was already losing the argument. She was hysterical and he just looked so reasonable. "I'm worried for her, too," he assured her. That was maybe the most frustrating part - he was Bettan's friend, just like she was. Nearly everyone was. He'd known her longer than Efa had. "But no one will take this seriously. It happens all the time."

"I don't see why we don't stop it," she said.

"Do you think I haven't asked about it?"

"And?"

"We get along so well with the humans. No one wants to change that. And lots of girls just end up happily married. It would be insulting them to act like this is a crime."

"They don't all end up happy," Efa said. There were selkies who came home ten years, twenty years later, their sealskin won back, and never spoke of what had happened while it was kept from them. There were mothers so determined not to be trapped that they abandoned their sons and daughters. Efa knew people, a dozen of them at least, who stayed away from their human forms forever out of fear that their sealskin might be taken again. She couldn't imagine losing one world to save the other, but they did it, and trembled at the thought of shedding their sealskins. "What's the point of getting along with humans if it means putting up with things like this?"

"You're not thinking," he said. She couldn't tell if he was angry with her. "We live right next to them. We trade with them, half the time we marry them. If we decided to pick a fight with humans, it would destroy us."

"Fishwives fight with humans," she said. It was a bad argument. She wasn't even sure if fishwives were real or just in stories, though either way they frightened her. "They drag them under and destroy their ships and eat them."

"Fishwives," he said, like just the word left him incredulous, "have to live in the middle of the deep sea, else the humans would root them out and burn every man, woman and child alive." Rees wasn't normally so violent in his language. She found herself folding her flippers in close to her body. There was something about him lately, the way he carried the weight of his adulthood, that made him hard to be around. They were none of them who they had been, and what was there for her to do about that?

He got up on his flippers and touched her with his nose. "I'm fine," she said. "I'm just scared for her."

"We'll look for her tomorrow," he promised. "It would just be embarrassing to bother people with this."

Rees was right about asking for help. Even if Bettan's sealskin had been stolen, which everyone admitted seemed like the most likely explanation, plenty of girls managed to turn that unhappy event into a full and fruitful life. Besides, her family didn't seem to be at all bothered by her absence.

Rees helped her search the village, though neither of them were very good at it. Nobody had heard much of anything. People promised, smiling, that if Bettan were to show up in their neighborhoods, they'd be very quick to hear about it - "She's not much one to stay quiet, is she?" - and just as quick to let Efa know.

George said he'd keep an eye out, but he also warned her not to hold out too much hope. There were hundreds of families in the town itself, and hundreds more in the open land surrounding it. "If I were our lad," he said, frowning like he didn't like the prospect, "I'd take her as far inland as I could stand, go live with cousins in the country. Somewhere nobody recognized her face."

"I never thought of that," Efa whispered. Then her limbs went weak, and George had to come around the other side of the bar to steady her. The knowledge that her sealskin could be stolen at any moment, that she could be barred from the depths, was terrifying. It shook her, and left her bursting into strangled sobs even when she thought she had her fears under control. But being taken inland, where she would be unable to smell the rich salt air, where the only water she could step into would be mucky and full of frog spawn - that was dizzying.

"You okay, girl?" George had one hand on each of her arms, ready to catch her in a dead faint. He so obviously loved Bettan that she had never realized he might like her, too.

"I just need to sit," she said. "I've been on my feet all day."

Arm around her shoulders, he guided her behind the bar and found a stool for her to sit on. She held her shoulders in close to her neck and smoothed down her skirt. She felt suddenly cold. He stepped behind her and came back with a mug of beer. When she reached to get coins out of her bag, he shook his head. "You look like you need a drink," he said.

She took it with thanks and held it in both hands. He leaned against the bar and watched her. Things were quiet this time of day, with only a few men in the inn nursing their drinks, so he could afford to ignore them. After she'd finished half of it, he said, "Feeling better?"

"A little," she said. "It's just - we're never going to find her like this, are we?"

George frowned. "We might. But maybe it's time for you to step back some."

She stared into her drink, willed strength into her body. "She wouldn't just give up, if it were me." Once Efa had broken her ankle exploring, and Bettan had half-carried her two hours back home. She'd stayed with her for weeks when Efa couldn't change back into her seal body or even walk anywhere, telling stories and (hesitantly, with a lot of grumbling) embroidering their dresses while Efa healed. Efa had no doubt that Bettan would do anything for her.

"I'm not saying to give up," he said, but his voice was quiet and he looked uncomfortable. "There's just not much left for you to do. Maybe she'll be able to find her own way out, or get a message to you."

She was already shaking her head before he finished talking. "That's a one-in-a-hundred chance. Hardly anyone escapes, unless they happen on their sealskin."

"She might. She's got pluck."

She looked at his shoes and didn't say anything.

He gave a great heaving sigh. "I didn't say it wasn't a long shot," he admitted. "I'm worried about you. You've done nothing else but look for her in days. I can't imagine you're eating, or sleeping for that matter."

She was only vaguely hungry, and could hardly relax enough to sleep, but she didn't think that would win him over. "I can't stand thinking of her out there with some stranger-"

"Who might be a perfectly nice young man," George said. "Some people think this is a very romantic way to start a marriage."

She made a sour face. "Not you, too."

"No. It's too much like kidnapping for me, and I have too many strong-willed daughters of my own. But he probably thinks so." He looked around the bar and said, steadily like that would make her believe him, "I know it looks bad, but I don't think she's in any danger."

She said, "We don't know that. He could be a monster." She gulped her beer and tried to ignore the way panic welled up in her whenever she thought too hard about this.

George squeezed her arm. "We'll find her, just you wait and see," he said. "We're bound to hear word eventually."

Efa's parents' house was large for a selkie home, with two rooms and a hearth. Most selkies wanted a building to protect their possessions; they had no need for entertaining, or a place to wait out the elements. But Efa's mother liked to cook and clean, and more to the point her father enjoyed having a wife who kept house. It wasn't nearly as grand as anything in the human town, and had been constructed piecemeal from scraps that Efa's father had bartered from the town's carpenters, but it was his love, and he had shepherded it through its creation with the same strength and constancy that had brought up his children. The result was imposing, and she always felt both proud and proper to look on it. She had grown up in a house, after all - not exactly as a human girl would have, for she was not human, but not, as some people would say, in "one of those selkie shacks," either.

She came into their home tired and with her teeth on edge, driven only by the feeling that she was still a child and ought to be by her parents. The house stood straight and steady, and her mother and father were inside. He sat in the light of the open window working on a leather bag; she was roasting whole crabs over the coals of the hearth.

Efa's mother was the first to look up. She was a stolid woman, but not ill-tempered, and she looked warmly on her daughter. "Would you like to stay?" she said. "It won't be ready for a while, but these are going to be soup. I can stretch them enough to fill your belly, too."

The warmth and the familiarity of it swept through Efa, the crackling of the hearth reaching her skin and dusting the cold off her shoulders. It straightened her back. "I'd love to," she said, and came forward to kiss both her parents. "What's in the soup?"

"Some of this, some of that," Efa's mother said. On the table sat a pile of ingredients - root vegetables, mostly, hearty stuff, the kinds of crooked parsnips it was easy to get off a farmer, the small green onions that grew wild in the forest.

"Your father got me a pot of cream when he was in town this morning, and of course I made him catch me some crab for his trouble."

Her father laughed. "It was no bother," he said. "I knew you'd want the cream. It's almost too late in the season for it."

Efa sat by her father at the table and wished she'd brought something to occupy her hands. Both her parents had taught her young that it was important to make something of herself. It came easily to Rees, his bold words and clear voice, the way he was at the same time what he wanted and what everyone else wanted. It was harder for Efa. She was happiest when she was sitting with something in her hands, something on the fire, her people around her - that or when she was alone with Bettan, somewhere she didn't think they should be.

She turned to her father and held her hands outstretched. "What are you working on?"

He handed the bag to her. The leather was almost black, soft and buttery. He was in the process of decorating it, poking small holes into the outside layer with an awl so that he could stitch through them later. It wasn't common for a selkie to take up a trade or a craft, more because it was unnecessary than because it was forbidden, but Efa's father liked to keep busy, he liked the feeling of having money that he had earned.

Efa angled the bag in her hands to better see the pattern, stroked the dots. They were so small that they could hardly be said to be there at all - it was fine work, and he only needed to be able to pass a few lines of coarse thread through the holes. But the shapes they formed were distinct swirls that curved and fell together. It was the sea in winter, the guttering gusts of wind and the moment before the break of a wave.

"It's beautiful," she said, and handed it back.

He smiled down at his handiwork. "Isn't it? People complain sometimes - 'Delwyn, my lad, does it have to be the ocean again?'"

"'Put some nice flowers on the next one,'" Efa's mother chimed in.

"But I tell them, you buy from a selkie, you have to know he's only got two loves. And I'm not putting my wife and kids on a bag!"

Efa laughed and tugged at the hem of her sleeve. "Have you heard about Bettan?" she asked.

Her mother sobered. It didn't take much. "Rees told us," she said.

Efa wasn't surprised. As a child, when she had been afraid to say something, she had told Rees. He had always been able to put it into words better than she could. "Everyone says I shouldn't be upset."

Her mother reached into the fire and flipped the crabs with a bit of cloth to spare her fingers the worst of the damage. They were good-sized crabs, and their shells were starting to blush and gleam. "Of course you're upset," she said. "She's your best friend, and now she's moved on to something else."

"I don't think that's it," Efa said. But she knew it was part of it. "Just, doesn't it seem like stealing to you? When a man takes a girl's sealskin? I don't think it's right."

She wasn't supposed to state it in so many words. She knew because her parents paused, lips pursed, and looked at each other.

"It isn't ideal," her mother said. At the same time, her father said, "I can see this is troubling you."

They looked at each other again. Efa's mother stood and walked over to her husband. She wrapped her arms around his lean shoulders as a young sweetheart might, and kissed the top of his balding head. When she spoke, it was in the tone of both a mother telling her children a grand tale and one trying to spare them a great fright. "We have been this way," she said, and her husband stilled his work to hear her words, "since there have been selkies."

Efa opened her mouth expecting to say something rude, but the words fell apart in her lips. There had been a time when she had had no patience for her mother, when she had been both short and sharp even without trying. But she was grown now, and they had both learned that a mother and a daughter each have nothing without the other. "Are you saying that it was meant to happen?" she asked. Humans believed in such things, but she had never heard it from another selkie.

Her mother shook her head. "I'm saying that we get to be part of the waves. And the exchange for that - there's always something, Efa, you know I taught you that - is that we have to take this risk."

Her father reached across the table and patted Efa's arm. "It's natural, love," he said. "Trying to fix it would be like trying to save those crabs your mother's cooking. It's their time."

Efa got the impression that her mother thought that was perhaps a bit much to say, but she didn't do anything to contradict it. "Bettan was going to marry soon anyway," she said instead. "And it would have been a wild wedding, but it was going to happen. Now, was it bad of this man to take her sealskin? I don't know. But if nothing happens that she wouldn't have done in her own time anyway, then there's nothing for any of us to mourn."

Efa was a practical girl. She could see the sense in that. But she couldn't help feeling unmoored. "What if he traps her? In a house somewhere inland, where you can't see the sea for days and she has to eat mutton?"

Her mother's smile was kind. "There are worse things than mutton," she said, which was no comfort.

"I think," said Efa's father, "you underestimate the power a wife has in her marriage. If your mother seemed unhappy, I'd do anything to fix it. Even men who aren't much good feel that way about the women they love."

"They might be strangers," Efa said.

He said, "Bettan's an easy girl to love. If he took her for his wife, he must have seen that."

Efa's mother hummed agreement. "And soon they'll have children," she said. "That changes everything, you'll see."

It was a pronouncement; there was nothing that could be said to that. Efa nodded glumly and helped to chop vegetables for the soup. She tried not to think of Bettan, far away, helping to roast a lamb for her own wedding day feast.

Bettan's father's name was Owen. Her mother was Seren.

She was an arch woman with a crooked nose and glossy hair curling to almost the tops of her thighs; it was blacker than the sky at night, with streaks of silver slipping their way down. When she wore her sealskin, which was more often than not, it was the same impossible color, and sleek. She had been born down the coast quite a ways, on an island where the humans did not often come, and had left only because her husband had wanted to raise their child where he had grown up.

It was hard to say if she regretted that decision. Certainly she and Owen got along, but she barely spoke to anyone else, except to tell the children haughtily of her home, how it had been beautiful and warm, how the grains of sand, when observed closely, had come in the shape of stars.

Efa was terrified of her. Bettan, who had inherited her looks, her way with men, and her temper, had never seemed to notice that Seren existed.

Rees helped her find them. He knew everyone's little hiding spots, and he'd known Bettan's parents since he was very small. They were out further in the sea than most people would go casually - Bettan had inherited her boldness from her mother, her love of adventure from her father.

"Yes, we'd heard about Bettan," Owen said, and Efa sensed his disapproval. "She is our daughter. We noticed that she was gone."

Efa didn't think there was any reason that they would notice. Bettan could go without seeing her parents for twice as long as Efa could. Once she'd gotten a horrible black eye in a fight and it had healed right up before her parents even caught a glimpse of it. But that was why she had brought her brother.

"We were hoping you would help us," Rees said. But he didn't get a response.

"To find her," Efa clarified. She tried to look as though she had a clue what she was doing, but she felt very young and very foolish. A fish caught Seren's eye, and she dove for it and ate it up while they watched.

Owen didn't speak until his wife had returned. "If she was taken," he said, and Efa suspected that he didn't disagree with that theory but was too stubborn to state anything as fact that had not been proven to him, "it was by a human. My wife and I, we don't leave the sea."

Rees made a soft noise that startled Efa, for it was very like a scowl. Their family, starting with their parents, was very genteel, very respectable. Efa had no doubt that her mother could have gone off and become a princess, dressed herself in brocade and jewels, if only she had not so loved the sea. And her father was an honest man, the kind of man who could hold his head high in any company, the kind of man who protected his children and made them proud to be of his line.

It was no surprise to anyone that Rees, tall, eloquent Rees, was the result of that pairing. Bettan's parents were not like that.

Oh, not that anyone especially disliked them.

At least, not Owen.

But they were seals more than anything. When they took off their sealskins, they wore scraps of clothing borrowed from their neighbors and never returned. They didn't go into town. Seren knew how to neither cook nor clean nor mend nor keep house at all. They didn't own much of anything, not even to share with others, and as far as they were concerned they didn't need to. Efa hadn't realized it at the time, but most of Bettan's human ways had come from Rees and from their parents. Efa's mother had sewn her dresses, Efa's father had pressed coins into her hands and told her to have fun in town. They had both given her little chores, little bits of advice, things she swore she didn't need but accepted handily.

Rees disapproved of the whole lot of it. He liked when things were done right, and he liked when the girls in his life - of which Bettan was certainly one - were treated with care and decorum.

"Please," Efa said. "She wouldn't have wanted this, she cares so much about her independence."

Seren made a soft, resigned noise, and Efa knew there would be no help from her. "My dear," she said, "I've always liked you. You're a good girl. You respect your elders, you do the right thing."

Rees hummed his agreement. Efa said, "Thank you, ma'am."

"Maybe it would have been easier," Seren said, "if you were my daughter."

(Bettan had said much the same thing. "They like me," she'd admitted, "but not as much as you." And she'd confessed, when she was feeling weepy and teenage and quite unloved, that she couldn't bring herself to listen to parents who had never cared for her. But as far as Efa knew, that was just her impression. They'd never actually said anything to support it.)

"I don't understand," she said. Beside her, she could feel her brother's outrage - and his hurt, as though it were his own mother speaking so of him.

Seren floated over and bumped against Efa's side. It was both affectionate and domineering. "Maybe when you're older," she said, and then seemed to acknowledge that that wasn't an answer. "Efa, it's hard. When you have a son, I imagine you expect that he'll make trouble for you. But with a daughter, you have things that you want from her. Things happen that you don't plan for, when you're young and in love."

"We were very excited to have a child," Owen added - quickly, like it would pardon them.

"But she didn't turn out," Seren said, "the way we had expected."

Rees must have seen her face, even though she was trying not to look at him, when they stepped onto the shore and shed their sealskins. She stood tall and walked slowly up the beach into the village. He came up beside her and draped his sealskin over her shoulders, put his arm around her to hold it in place.

"This way," he said, tugging her down a side path rather than straight into the village. "You don't want to have to talk to somebody else right now."

"I'm fine," she said. She had never, even in the wildest throes of youth, struggled to put on a good face, to be sociable, to fit into her place in the village.

But he was right that her constancy, the part of her that was sweet and warm and good all the way through, like the small loaves of molasses bread their mother made for holidays, was a frayed thing. If she had met someone, even someone she liked, who had known her from a pup and protected her from currents too strong for her, she would have smiled, and her voice would have been cheerful. But they would have seen the strain, and they would have worried.

"I know you are," he said, and for all that Efa heard the condescension in his voice she didn't feel condescended to. "Come on, we'll get you sat down out of the way and then I'm going to make this right."

He sounded both like his old self and like a man. His sealskin was heavy on her shoulders, as she knew surely it must be on his. She ducked her head against his side and let him lead her into the thin forest beside the village. The trees were wispy, with pale gray bark and leaves shaped like eyes. They weren't of a size for building houses, not like the trees on the mainland, so they had been left untouched. He took her deep into the woods, far enough that she could have screamed without fear that anyone would hear her, but the leaves of the trees and the brush were sparse enough that they could almost see the shapes of the village.

She sat at the base of a tree, her back straight against its trunk and her head facing the ground. She sat with his sealskin around her and her sealskin in her lap. He took a perch on a flat rock and hummed the tunes to songs he wouldn't sing aloud.

Efa spread her sealskin out, examining it for tears or imperfections. It was impossible that she would have missed them, but not as impossible as it had been before. She felt the shape of her flippers, the smooth line up her back, the eerie holes where her mouth and her eyes belonged. It was her body, and had never bothered her before, but suddenly she wondered how it would look to a human. Like treasure, perhaps, or just like any animal's pelt. Gruesome either way.

"I hate them," she said. It was the harshest thing she'd ever said about Bettan's parents, and she couldn't find any conviction in it.

Rees didn't look up, or start. He had been waiting for her.

"They shouldn't get to call themselves selkies," she added treacherously, "if they don't care about what happens to her."

"You can't dismiss everyone you know so easily," he said. And, before her fury could overcome her sense that he was probably right, "Although you love her an awful lot for trying."

"If we were humans, we wouldn't be so afraid of trying to get her back," Efa said.

"Maybe," he agreed, "but we'd have to be humans."

"If we were wolves, we'd kill anyone who tried to hurt our pack."

He nodded and did not say, though it was true, that she knew nothing about wolves. What he did say was crueler. "And when wolves war with men, the men slaughter the lot."

She thought, but did not say: if we were fishwives, we would destroy half the world to find her, and then she would help us to destroy the rest. It was a crazy thought, and Rees, who loved her, did not have room in his life for that.

He was still talking. "We can't be anything but what we are," he said. She thought for the first time that his certainty of himself, that absolute sense he had of where he was and where his borders ended, the thing she had never had and had envied, might be a trap that held him. "We have to live our lives-"

"With good intent," she interrupted him fiercely. She had heard that speech before, more because he liked to give it than because he found her lacking. "We have to do right."

"With balance and caution," he said. "I know you care about her."

"I'm starting to wonder if you-"

"Don't." Rees sounded so horrified, and so firm, that she shut her mouth on the hateful things she had been about to say, and was surprised by them herself. "Don't you dare say that to me, like I don't love her. You'll never be able to take it back."

"I'm sorry," she said.

He didn't acknowledge it, but Efa knew he had heard. "We can't afford to make things worse," he said. "If we did what you wanted, we'd get Bettan back, all right. Probably you'd grab a knife and hold it to her poor suitor's throat."

Efa considered that, then nodded weakly. Certainly she knew her way around a work knife better than any real weapon.

He grimaced. There were times when she imagined his thoughts were too much for him, and he couldn't say everything. "We'd be such an easy target. It would be no harder than digging up clams."

"Well," she said, "we can't just give up on her."

It didn't matter to her that he was right. She was sure that he knew that, and that it killed him, and that he forgave her. "We'll find her," he said. "I don't know if we can do much more than that, but we'll find her."

Efa adjusted his sealskin around her shoulders, held it taut against her. "And what then?" she said. "What if she's miserable?"

It took him a long time to decide what he was going to say, but he held eye contact while he thought. "I don't know," he said. He stood and stooped to pull her to her feet. "Whatever we have to. But carefully."

She nodded, and she thanked him, and he walked her to her door, and they agreed that the next morning, they would start looking themselves.

That night, she left to find the fishwives.

{ 2 }

SHE DIDN'T KNOW WHERE SHE WAS GOING. All that she knew of where she might find the fishwives was what she had been told. They ranged everywhere, but only infrequently. They seemed to like warm waters and the cold depths. They were often found by wrecks, either because they caused them or because they liked to pick fresh meat from the bones. She'd always been a good navigator, but until now that had only meant she could find her way home.

She moved away, towards what felt like safety, and told herself that it was instinct.

When she first saw the fishwife, Efa didn't believe it. Nothing in her life had ever moved like that before. She was big, just her tail longer than Efa's whole body from nose to hind flippers, and fast. She moved not like a human or a seal, as Efa had assumed, or even like a fish, but almost like an eel, her body ribboning out from behind her head.

All Efa's instincts told her to turn around now, while she had yet to catch the fishwife's attention, and swim away as fast as she could. And it wasn't just the animal part of her that thought that. She was realizing, now that she actually saw the beast, that everything she knew about fishwives she had learned from stories. Human stories, usually, and most of them so murky with a sailor's bravado that she could barely recognize them in the creature before her. There had never been any reason to trust that an encounter with a fishwife would end well.

But she'd been swimming by herself for days, and nothing had gone horribly wrong yet. (That argument was not as persuasive or as comforting as she needed it to be.) She couldn't just leave.

"Hey!" she called in Sealish, slapping the water.

The fishwife stopped. For a second, Efa thought that she might bolt. Then she turned and swam slowly closer.

It was what she'd wanted, but her stomach still clenched with nerves to see something so big swimming towards her. She took a breath, determined not to panic, and shed her sealskin.

When she blinked her human eyes open, the fishwife was only an arm's length away, watching her. Efa clutched her sealskin against her body. There wasn't anyone around to mind her nakedness - the fishwife, she could see now, had made no such concessions - but she had spent enough time among humans to make her modest.

The fishwife said something. Her teeth were sharp and numerous between her dark, full lips. Efa swallowed and opened her mouth to speak before she realized she hadn't caught a single word.

"I'm sorry," she said. "I don't understand you."

They tried three more languages before one, a trade tongue a good girl wouldn't have known, finally stuck. The fishwife licked her top teeth and smiled. "Yes," she said, "this will work."

This close, she was beautiful. Legend said that selkies were beautiful, too, and Efa supposed they were, with their strong legs and liquid eyes. But not like this girl, whose fingers came to wicked points and whose hair was a tangle like seaweed at low tide. She moved under the waves and the sun glinted off the tiny silver scales of her tail.

She was staring. The fishwife made a little noise in the back of her throat. "You're not a siren," she said.

Efa laughed and shook her head. "Are you allowed to talk to people who aren't fishwives? Er, I mean-"

"Either word is fine. No, there's not a rule." Something about her suggested that if there had been, she probably would have ignored it. "I just don't."

"I'm not human, either," she said. The fishwife raised her eyebrows and looked over Efa's barely covered body. "I'm a selkie. It means - I can be a seal, but I don't have to."

Her lips moved silently, like she was thinking. "I've never heard of it."

That was just Efa's luck, too. She would find a fishwife, and one who looked to be about her age, who was a skeptic. "Well, we exist," she said, smiling broad and nervous.

The fishwife nodded once. Often when humans saw a selkie change for the first time, they didn't believe it, they didn't trust themselves. This woman didn't necessarily believe Efa, but she seemed to trust her own eyes. "You say there are more of you?" she said sidelong.

"Not here," Efa said. "Back home. Days away." Part of her cringed at admitting how vulnerable she was, without even her brother to keep an eye on her, but she didn't want to look like a threat. Those fingernails looked like they were made to rip skin, and she didn't think the teeth were for show, either.

The fishwife relaxed minutely. Efa had made the right gamble. "Why would a little selkie girl be so far away from her people?"

"I'm grown," she protested. Then blushed, because she didn't sound it. This was the point where, according to the plan, she was supposed to explain everything. The plan seemed to be falling apart under this woman's gaze.

"Just as long as no one comes thinking I stole you," the fishwife said. Efa didn't mention that the only thing protecting them from that fate was that no one would ever suspect she'd go so far from the coast. There were probably still people looking for her, but they'd be searching the islands and the villages.

"No, I wouldn't worry about that," she said, pushing away her guilt. "I wanted to see what was out here, is all."

The fishwife was silent for a long while, and Efa hoped she didn't look as implausibly adventurous as she felt. "All right," she said. She looked over her shoulder to the wide ocean, something delicate on her face. "Come and I'll show you."

The fishwife's name was Ninka. She said it short and fast, so that Efa had to ask four times for her to repeat herself. She took them off somewhere that seemed to Efa like just another patch of ocean, but that Ninka apparently knew. Efa wasn't sure what she was using for landmarks. For days Efa had been using guesswork and, when she could, the stars.

This time when Efa shed her sealskin to talk, Ninka stayed close by and watched. Usually humans were too unnerved to look, and selkies had seen the process enough times that they didn't care. Ninka stared like she didn't trust what Efa might turn into if she wasn't supervised.

"Where are we?" Efa asked when she was done, although Ninka didn't have the manners to stop staring at her. She wished that she had been able to bring a dress, though it wouldn't have done her much good in the water. She'd been so desperate to escape that she hadn't actually prepared.

"You wanted to see around," Ninka said. Efa wondered if that excuse sounded as flimsy as it did to her, but there wasn't any way to say - what? That she wanted to learn to be a monster? That the only thing worse than what had happened to Bettan was that they were both helpless? "And I like it here. It's so calm."

She could see nothing but water in all directions and the waves that lifted them up and set them back down again. Ninka was constantly in motion, her tail whirling in spirals to keep her afloat. Efa was curvier; she could just lean back on her shoulders and be buoyed by the waves. "Does that mean nothing's going to..." She groped for words. "Come after us?"

"'Come after us'?" Ninka repeated. "You mean, like a shark?" Then she seemed to realize that Efa was serious, and scared, because she said, briskly, "No, of course not. Would I take us somewhere dangerous?"

She looked like something out of every terrifying tale Efa had ever been told as a child. People like her destroyed ships and left their inhabitants to drown without a thought. (That was exactly what Efa was looking for, but she still had to try hard not to be frightened of it.) "We only just met," Efa said, trying to be polite.

Ninka laughed with all her teeth. "And you're only a little seal. Well, there's nothing around here that I can't handle." She flexed her hands, and Efa believed her. "You're not one for the ocean, are you?"

"What do you mean?" she said. "I love water."

Ninka shrugged. "You keep looking around like you expect something to bite you."

There was that. She combed through her hair with her fingers as she spoke. "I've never been out so far until now. Maybe other selkies live where it's deep, but we - my village - we stay close to the shore."

"But you came all the way out here for a little adventure."

"I wanted to see if I could find fishwives," Efa said. She hated to lie, even when the truth wouldn't get her what she wanted. "I heard you stayed in the deep so the humans couldn't get to you."

That sent Ninka into a fit of giggles. "No one ever thinks maybe we just like it here, do they?" She didn't wait for an answer. "That's it, really? You came out here looking for me?"

The way she asked it, with a tiny smile, made Efa think that she had to answer very carefully. "That's about it," she said.

Ninka was delighted. She grinned and relaxed and made a soft high-pitched noise to herself. "Well then, Efa the selkie," she said, still laughing, "I hope this is everything you've ever wanted."

They went hunting together and each was pleasantly surprised by the other's skill. Efa had tried to catch fish in her human body before, and it was a painful, thankless task that always left her feeling slow and clumsy. Ninka moved so quickly Efa could barely follow what she was doing. She caught fish by biting into them and tearing off the rest of their squirmy bodies with her claws. Then she held them in her hands and, grinning, finished them off the way Efa might have eaten a pickle: raw, in a series of big bites starting at the head and working her way down.

"I thought I was going to have to help you at first," she told Efa when they were done. It was dark by then, and Efa was watching the stars come out.

"I've been feeding myself for years, you know."

"It's just that you're so slow," she said, and didn't even duck when Efa splashed her. "I was shocked when you caught that big one. Up until then I'd been thinking selkies, they're cute but pretty useless."

Efa sputtered. "We're not useless," she insisted. "We're just not the biggest, baddest things around. You should see my brother, he's the best fisher I know."

"You've been mentioning him a lot," Ninka said. (Efa flushed. Bettan had always said that she talked too much about other people, especially her brother, when she was nervous.) "Why didn't you take him with you, if he's so great?"

She was smiling; Efa was pretty sure that she was teasing her. She felt vaguely guilty anyway. The smart thing to have done would have been to have accepted her brother's help and kept looking. It was just that she'd tried that, and it hadn't worked, and she'd gotten desperate, and - and fishwives destroyed sailors' ships just for fun. She had wanted to be among people who didn't shut up and fall in line as soon as a human started talking. But now she was relaxing with this beautiful, deadly woman who didn't even know Bettan existed.

She couldn't just tell her and beg for help. Efa was starting, slowly, to get an impression of Ninka as they spent time together, and the thing that stuck out most was that anyone who accepted her charity would have to bleed for it. She would just have to wait until, soon enough probably, she got taken to the other fishwives. Then she could ask an adult, someone as bloodthirsty as Ninka but more approachable, for help. And then (Ninka fussed with her hair, claws dipping behind her ear and trailing down her neck; Efa smiled) they would help her strategize.

"He's not really an adventurer," she said, looking out over the ocean lit up by the moon. "He's, you know, he cares a lot about our village and the community. He's a big leader. I don't think he'd leave them for anything." She'd always had visions of Rees as a general in battle, like in those old stories, or a king. People would do anything he asked of them because they knew he'd do anything for them. She was just proud, and glad it wasn't her. "Do you have a brother or a sister?"

Ninka seemed unsure. "I suppose I do," she finally said. "I hadn't considered it."

She'd never gotten that answer before. "Not very close?" she asked.

"Oh, we're close enough." She made a dismissive motion with her hand. "Are families very, um, important to selkies?" She still said the word like she wasn't sure she believed in it.

"Of course!" Efa said, high-pitched. They were certainly important to her. "Your family's all you've got. That and your village, but they're really just more family."

"It's not that way for us," she said, quietly, as though trying not to disappoint.

"I mean, we're not as bad as humans. We usually leave our families once we're grown. They'll stay with their parents until they're ready to get married. That is, start a family themselves," she said, suddenly realizing that she had no idea how much Ninka knew about basic life concepts.

"I know what marriage is," Ninka said. "A human boy even wanted to make me his wife, once."

Efa flipped herself off her back and stared at Ninka, at her slim body ringed with weapons. She looked half fish, and not just her tail, either. Men so often balked at the realization that Efa and Bettan weren't human, and they were perfectly normal girls other than the seal thing. Ninka could never be mistaken for normal, not even if she took the seashells out of her hair and slipped on a nice gown. "He must have been awfully brave," she caught herself saying.

Bettan would have pouted prettily. Ninka bared her teeth in a silent laugh. "They love us," she said. "They think I'm beautiful." She had no more modesty than the sea itself.

"Is that why you speak so many languages? Talking to humans?"

"We must speak to each other, too. But yes, that helps. Sailors, mostly, and fishermen in their boats."

The water rose and knocked them together. Ninka took Efa's wrist, claws prickling on her skin, and pushed her away. Efa kicked herself farther and looked down at her sealskin. "Is it true that you wreck ships and drown the men in them?" Her voice was quiet, but carried well across the water.

"What do you think?"

She wasn't sure what she wanted to believe. She needed it to be real, so that she could get the help she needed, so that these people could teach her strength and she could save Bettan. But she liked Ninka. She didn't know that she could be close to someone who would do something so barbaric. "I think it's true," she said, finally, unhappy with her conclusion.

Ninka whistled, long and soft. "You're so quick to believe the worst of me," she said. She didn't sound particularly upset about it. "It happens sometimes, yes. But I've spared more men than I've eaten. I've been perfectly kind to you, haven't I?"

"You have," she agreed, and Ninka looked pleased. "Are there more of you around, or are you mostly alone?" She had an image of Ninka as a child, exploring the deep ocean by herself, without anyone to talk to. It felt wondrous and sad at the same time.

"There are lots of us. I just like it this way, so I only go looking for them every few days or so."

That made some sense, although it was hard for Efa to imagine going days without seeing another person and liking it. Just the trip out into the sea to seek out fishwives had left her near-crazed with loneliness. "But what do you do, if you're all by yourself?"

Ninka looked at her strangely. "Whatever I want. I go exploring, and fish, and bother sailors and seduce young women on the seashore."

Efa choked. "You what?"

"I sing," she said quickly, although it was hard to believe her. "But it's not a bad life, Efa. I never need to be alone." She wrinkled her nose. "Although often it's better."

"So you aren't always just the monster from the deep," she said. She was trying to reassure herself, maybe.

Because Ninka certainly didn't need that reassurance. "Of course not," she said. "Did you know they say that we're good luck?"

"Despite the drownings and everything?"

"Despite the drownings and stealing husbands everywhere we go," she agreed. Efa frowned. Selkies were accused of stealing men, too, with their steady natures and their beauty. A selkie wife would be strong and reliable, would cook up a storm and keep a house clean without a hint of complaint, would have no problems entrancing a man with her soft lips or pushing out babies through those sturdy hips. Now that she was old enough men watched her in the streets, now that her best friend had been taken to be one of those famed selkie wives, the whole mythology made her sick to her stomach. Ninka didn't notice. "We're good luck just as long as we like you."

The way she smiled, Efa thought - hoped - that she liked her.

They stayed up late whispering back and forth like little girls and listening to the waves. When the conversation quieted, Efa leaned back and let the sea carry her. Ninka sang songs she had never heard before, voice high and strong and beautiful, and that was what she thought of as she fell asleep that night.

Ninka loved the deep as much as it was possible for her to love anything. She took Efa to all of her favorite places and for a few days, they barely spoke. Efa could communicate, albeit only in Sealish, underwater, but Ninka found it hard to hide her distaste for the animal tongue.

"No," Ninka said, "watch me." And her hands moved, as fast and as hard to follow as a school of fish. Efa was entranced, but also revolted, because suddenly she was certain that Ninka had broken skin with those claws. "What do you think I just said?"

"Said?" She paused. "Do all fishwives talk with their hands?"

"We need to be able to speak underwater," Ninka said impatiently, "and quietly."

"We don't have anything like that where I'm from," Efa said, shaking her head nervously. Criminals, maybe, had hand-signals. Conmen and smugglers, she imagined, who needed to be able to do things without anyone else hearing about it. It wasn't the sort of thing a woman like her would get involved in.

Ninka's tail curled and hit the surface of the water hard. "Of course you do," she said. It was clear from her voice and her smile that she felt she was being very reasonable. "What do you do when someone can't talk?"

"They use Sealish. Even when we're born we know it - else how would a mother be able to talk to her baby before he can shed his sealskin?"

"Or can't hear."

"I don't know." Efa looked down. "I've never really thought about it."

Either Ninka's body was stronger against the pressure of the water, or she was better at pretending not to notice. Efa could dive deep, but when her chest was starting to feel as though it might be crushed, sure enough Ninka would wave her forward. Ninka took them down so deep that Efa could see that there were mountains on the ocean floor, complete with ravines, gaping cuts in the ground where the sea floor fell into an abyss. It was terrifying imagining what might be down there. Ninka loved it.

"Have you ever gone in?" Efa asked when they returned to the surface.

Ninka shook her head. "It's too deep, even for me. And can't you feel the currents? I'd be crushed, or swept away." But she said it like she couldn't imagine anything better.

Ninka took her to giant forests of seaweed, tall and swaying in the waves, with small fish and sea creatures everywhere, and they played hide and seek. She took them to places where there was no light, and Efa had to go off of what she could feel with her whiskers. Ninka could see clearly at almost any depth, though her eyes looked almost the same as any human girl's. She took Efa to a bay and they swam upstream to look at the boats and the strange people who lived in the city on the water - although not for long, because a few hours in fresh water turned Ninka's skin ashen and her voice raspy.

She told Efa stories ("I'll take you there," she said, "only it's far, and I don't quite know the way,") of underwater volcanoes, places where the ground opened up and molten earth poured out into the sea. Stories of fish the size of cities, with long arched backs and mouths that gaped wide enough to swallow the sun. Stories of storms, of wrecks so bad that chests of jewels and of men were split open and strewn amongst the waves.

"Don't cry," Ninka said piteously, wiping Efa's face with the backs of her claw-studded fingers. "They were dead, they were long dead, there was nothing I can do."

Efa sniffed and splashed some water on her face. "But their families-"

"If you give your life to the sea, your family stops mattering," Ninka said.

Efa didn't believe that. She'd seen fishermen dizzy with relief that they'd survived a storm, that they'd made it back to their wives and babies. "So you just loot?" she said. "Is that where you got that?"

Ninka grabbed the necklace she wore and examined it. It was a gaudy thing, a heavy chain of ruddy gold that held a garnet pendant the size of a man's thumbnail, and easily worth more than all the jewels in Efa's village combined. When selkies had finery - and often they liked to - it was bits of ribbon, bits of leather, shells strung on a cord.

Ninka didn't answer the question. "I like beautiful things," she said, "and fish. There's nothing wrong with that."

"It is beautiful," Efa said.

"Really?" Ninka said. She looked suddenly shy. "Do you like it? You can have it."

"Oh, no!" Ninka was already starting to pull the necklace over her head; Efa reached out and pushed her hand back down. "It - it's too much. It wouldn't suit my complexion." And she realized, to her surprise, that she liked the way it looked just below the hollow of Ninka's throat.

"Just follow me through here," Ninka said a few days later. "It gets a little tight, but if I can make it through, you can."

They had managed to pull together a shaky system of communication despite all of the obvious problems. Efa swam better in her seal form, and preferred it overall - although, she had to admit, less so now that she was spending her days with someone who couldn't speak Sealish and expected her to understand sign. But they were well-matched. Efa was a little bit slower, but Ninka couldn't hold her breath in a dive for as long. For the most part, Ninka talked and they both assumed that Efa was willing to go along with it.

She was, however, uncertain about what "a little tight" meant. They were at the edge of an island (one of the beautiful tropical islands Ninka had been showing her, with forests Efa was sure counted as jungles, and strange animals like something out of a story) and Ninka had promised that they were about to tour her favorite cave. Efa was okay with caves, in theory. There weren't very many around her home, and those that she and Bettan had been able to find were shallow at best. She bopped Ninka's arm with her nose and made uncertain noises.

Ninka laughed. "Exactly. It'll be great," she said. They needed to work on her seal noise interpreting skills.

Then, with a leap, Ninka dove underwater and straight into the cliff face that made up this side of the island. At the last minute, just when Efa was sure she was going to smash her skull into the rocks and die, she slipped into a crevice.

A crevice.

Efa wasn't even sure why she followed, except that she had years of following Bettan faithfully under her belt and she knew if she didn't she'd never hear the end of it. The opening in the rocks, more like a tunnel than a crevice, though too jagged and rough to have been done intentionally, got narrower before it opened up. Efa had no idea how Ninka managed to squeeze her body through it when she barely fit. But finally she was released into an underground lake, and she followed Ninka to the surface.

Ninka waited patiently while she got changed into her human form and caught her breath. "How did you even find this?" Efa said, blinking as her eyes adjusted. The water was deep, but a lip of rock had formed over it, extending into the darkness. Somewhere ahead of them, off in the distance a ways, was a crack in the ceiling. Through it streamed the only light Efa could see. "You barely even fit. You must have been sure you were going to die, the first time."

It was hard to see Ninka, almost perfectly still in the calm water. "I'm not afraid of much," she said.

Efa put her sealskin down on the rock and swam closer, so close that she could hear Ninka breathe, even if she could only barely make out her face. "I'm starting to realize that," she said.

Ninka made a little noise in the back of her throat. "I'm really glad I met you," she said.

"Me, too."

That seemed to be the answer she had been looking for, because she took Efa's face in both of her hands and kissed her.

Her lips were cold but smooth, and her hands were surprisingly gentle, for all that those were claws tangled in the roots of Efa's hair. She pulled away quickly, stroking the line of Efa's cheekbone with her thumb. Efa had no doubt that she knew exactly what she was doing. And other than that, well, it was hard to think at all.

Ninka held her close, waiting for a reaction. Water ran in rivulets from her fingers down the sides of Efa's face. Efa swallowed and licked her lips. This close, half-nervous half-anticipatory, Ninka was magnificent. Efa never wanted to leave. And then she froze.

Her best friend was trapped as some awful man's wife and here she was, cavorting with a fish girl.

She grabbed Ninka's arms as if to push her away or to hold her there, but she didn't do either. "I'm sorry," she said, "where I'm from - people like me, we don't do this."

"Don't kiss?" Ninka said, smile disarming. "But it's so much fun."

Efa pushed her hands away and didn't miss them one bit. "Don't kiss people we just met. Don't sneak off into caves where we might get ourselves killed. Don't kiss like it's just, I don't know, some joke."

"I thought it was a nice cave. We're the only ones who even know it exists."

"And certainly," Efa said, voice trembling, "don't kiss girls."

"I'm sorry," Ninka said. She had sunk into the water up to her chin. "I didn't realize."

"Did I look like I wanted that sort of thing?"

"I thought you liked me," she said.

Efa couldn't bring herself to make eye contact. "I do," she said. Even the kissing hadn't been as far from what she wanted as she felt it should have been. She had never been kissed before - not really kissed, anyway. She'd been grabbed by drunk men looking to plant a big wet smacker on her lips, but that wasn't the same as being kissed with intent. Now that she had been, she was starting to revise her opinion that Bettan was crazy for liking it. "It's just that I'm not here to fool around."

She wanted to scream, she was so disappointed in herself. She had come looking for fishwives with a serious plan to ask for help and get home as quickly as possible. A few days, a week or two at most, just as long as she needed to get there, persuade them to help her, come up with a plan, and come back. (She'd hoped to learn some secret weapon, but she'd discarded the notion as soon as she'd seen Ninka. With a body like that, no one needed weapons.) And despite all her best intents, she'd frittered away the past few days with her new friend. She was a traitor, as surely as if she'd replaced Bettan altogether.

"Then I don't think you've been honest with me," Ninka said. "Because a grand adventurer wouldn't be bothered by the occasional... diversion."

Efa swam up to the edge of the rock and clambered up on out of the water. She'd rather liked the idea of herself as a wanderer, looking only for new experiences, but she could only pretend so long when Bettan was waiting for her. "Something awful happened in my town," she explained. "You have to understand, I couldn't tell you."

"Perfectly," Ninka said. Efa had never seen her in a sulk before.

"I'm sorry," she said.

"Whatever." She leaned back into the water like she was just too exasperated with the world to cope. "Do I get to know why you're really here?"

Efa curled up into a little ball on the rocks, her arms around her knees. "Bettan - my best friend - had her sealskin stolen."

"So she can't be a seal any more?" Ninka said.

"Yeah. And she has to marry the guy who stole it. So she's gone, and-" She took a breath to steady her voice. "-I need to get her back."

"I thought you all liked marriage."

Efa laughed hopelessly. "That's why I'm here myself. Everyone thinks she's going to be fine, but - I mean, would you want to marry some man you didn't even know? Just because he kidnapped you?"

Ninka was quiet for a moment. "I wouldn't want to marry a man," she said, "but I suppose you know that now."

Efa hadn't guessed that one, not exactly, but it made sense. Ninka was so independent, maybe she would be happier if she stayed single for the rest of her life. Efa couldn't imagine it for herself, but had a lot of practice being supportive when her friends did things she couldn't imagine. "She's like you," she said, because that was the best way she could think to explain it. "She's miserable with anyone around telling her what to do. She needs to marry a man who knows that and just lets her do what she wants. Someone who loves her for who she is." Efa had spent a lot of time thinking about how to get Bettan happily paired off.

"So why doesn't she just leave?" Ninka asked. She had come closer, although not nearly as close as she'd been before, and was resting her elbows on the rock.

"Because he's got her sealskin," she said.

"So?"

She felt a sensation quite like vertigo. "You can't just leave your sealskin," she said. "You're born with it, it'd be like - like leaving a leg behind on a whim, except worse because you can do just fine without a leg!"

"I think so, anyway," Ninka said.

"Besides, she literally can't. If someone's got your sealskin, you have to do what they want. No one knows why, it's just how it's always been."

"So," Ninka said, smiling, "if I had your sealskin, and I said, 'Go get me all the fish in the sea,' you'd have to do it?"

She was joking, and Efa felt like she should laugh, but it wasn't funny like that. "No, no, it's a lot more basic than that. I mean, it has to be, everyone says it's as old as whatever magic let us take off our sealskins in the first place. It's - he won't be able to make her cook whatever he likes for dinner each night, but if he wants her to stay with him, or go along with what he tells her to do, she won't have a choice."

Ninka actually shuddered at that. Efa felt relieved and no less alone. "And they think we're horrible just because we kill people occasionally," Ninka said.

"For fun," Efa reminded her, feeling tired. "You kill people occasionally for fun."

"Are you even sure you want to rescue her?" Ninka asked the next day.

"Uh, yes." She was quickly realizing that Ninka's moral code was not at all equivalent to her own. "Why?"

"Well, it's just it sounds like losing your sealskin is a dangerous thing, is all," she said. "Do you want to do that to yourself?"

"I'll hide it really well," Efa said. She thought that she was never going to let her sealskin out of sight again. She could do mending for weeks until she had enough money to buy another bag, one bigger than the one she already had, and then she'd carry it with her everywhere she went. "I'm only in danger if they take it, after all."

Ninka shook her head. "I'm just saying, how hard could it possibly be to find a new best friend?"

Another time she said, "Why did you come all the way out here looking for fishwives anyway? You could have just gone to save her yourself."

"Because I'm not a genius strategist," Efa said, shaking her head. "I needed someone to help me figure out what I was doing. I'd heard all the stories about what you do to ships, and I thought-"

"So you were just looking for a ruthless killer?"

Efa blushed. She didn't like to think of it like that. "I guess so."

"Then it's a good thing you found me, isn't it?"

She couldn't answer that. "You don't understand. Back home nobody fights anything, it's like they're all just willing to sit back and let some guy we don't even know take her, just because he wants to."

"And you thought we'd do better?" Ninka said.

"You will, right?"

"I think so." Ninka wasn't usually uncertain, so this didn't help Efa's nerves about the whole endeavor. "I've never had problems with people taking advantage of me, anyway." Efa, who had always been the gullible one, always the butt of practical jokes, always the one who had to stay and do chores while the the other kids snuck off to play, wanted to say, obviously you haven't. Ninka was too pretty for that, or maybe just too scary. "You might have forgotten one tiny detail, though."

"What's that?"

"How are we supposed to save your friend when there's no way for us to get up on land?"

Efa ducked her whole body underwater in protest. "I don't need you to come up with me," she said, even though it would have been nice to have been able to ask. She had suspected from the beginning that if anyone were to save Bettan it would be her, and she would be lucky to get any support. "That's not why I came at all. I just need help - a plan, some training. Some ideas."

"You're crazy," Ninka said. And, "This friend of yours probably doesn't deserve all the trouble you're going to for her." And, "How can I help?" And sometimes she just looked at Efa in a way she couldn't read, but that made her feel like she was about to be devoured. (When Ninka looked at her like that, she was left smiling and wishing she didn't have to spend all her time worrying about Bettan.) But even though Ninka didn't agree it was necessary, she accepted that rescuing Bettan was important to Efa. And, with a self-deprecating smile and a murmured "I'm not exactly a soldier, either," she agreed to take Efa to meet the rest of her people.

{ 3 }

I T TOOK ALMOST A DAY TO GET FROM WHERE THEY WERE
TO THE PART OF THE OCEAN NINKA REFERRED TO AS THE
"THRONE ROOM." The water was pale blue, warm and
shallow there. Efa had spent her entire life by the ocean, but
she'd never known it to be anything other than cold and im-
petuous, a deep shade of blue-green. Where the fishwives
kept their society, the ocean reflected the light like a crystal
and the fish came in wild colors. Sharp black mountains rose
out of the sea and created a bay in the shape of a crescent; Efa
imagined they had carved it with their claws. "I like it out in
the deep," Ninka explained, "but it's easier to build things if
you're close to the trade routes." And indeed, the area the sirens had claimed for themselves was studded with islands,
most of them uninhabited, and easily full of ships.

The first thing, Ninka explained, was that they had to introduce Efa to the king. He would take offense if she just
showed up and started bothering all of his subjects without so
much as a by-your-leave. Efa combed her hair with her fingers and worried the whole way there.

"You'll be fine," Ninka said. "He'll be there, probably there'll be some other people around, you'll introduce your-self to him, we'll all go find something delicious to eat."

"Why do you have a king?" she asked. "I thought you did-n't want anything to do with humans."

"I don't," Ninka agreed. "But Idain likes it when people call him the king, and we do what he tells us to."

She didn't like the sound of that. "Can't we just meet with the prince instead?"

"What prince?"

"The heir, the second-in-command, whatever you call him."

Ninka was looking at her, head cocked, like there was something funny. "We don't have one of those. You're going to have to deal with the real guy."

Efa couldn't see how that would work. Society would inev-itably fail, without the stability of everyone knowing who came after the king. But she didn't think Ninka would care about that. She didn't seem very interested in society as a concept. "Well, I can't meet him naked."

"Don't see why not," Ninka said, but she helped Efa to tie her sealskin around her body in a way that covered most of the important bits. And then she explained the worst part - they had to go meet him underwater.

"I can't dive that long in this body," Efa said, starting to panic.

"Don't worry about it, it's not too deep. I'm sure he'll want to talk soon anyway."

The throne room turned out to be nothing of the sort. It was just a space on the ocean floor somewhat more cultivated than the rest of it, filled with fishwives and -husbands. There were fewer than twenty in all, and Efa wasn't sure if that was more or less than she had expected. It was less, anyway, than the Hungry Hogfish could hold on a good night. It was easy to pick Idain out of the crowd. He was wearing a crown of braided seaweed in his long hair, and even without it he was a sight to behold. Efa found herself memorizing each of his muscles so she could recount them to Bettan later. He looked about ten years older than they were, maybe a little more, and had a ruggedly handsome way about him. His chest and stomach were solid, with wicked curved scars every few handspans. He smiled to see Ninka, and they did a lot of bowing and uproarious, silent conversation before finally, just when Efa thought her lungs were going to give out, they all rose to the surface.

"It's certainly unconventional," Idain said by way of greeting. He swam right over to Ninka and brushed a kiss over her cheek. "I didn't expect you of all people to bring a human here."

"I like her," Ninka said. There were a dozen other sirens watching them blatantly, and even more doing their best to be sneaky. "And she's not a human, she's a selkie. She can wear that sealskin and transform herself."

Idain coughed and looked her over with more care. "Then it's an honor to meet you, Miss-"

"Efa," she said, and extended her hand. He stared at it for a moment, then took it with some awkwardness. "Just Efa is fine, Your Majesty."

"Idain, King of the Sea. What brings you here? It can't just be that Ninka thinks you're..." He seemed to struggle for words, lips quirked. "...intriguing."

She explained, as simply and concisely as she could, her problem, trying not to let herself get intimidated. She wasn't used to speaking to anyone important, but that was no excuse not to present herself well. "I was hoping that you could help."

His teeth, when he showed them, were as pointed as Ninka's and more straggly. "I'm not sure how much we can do for you, but it sounds like an interesting dilemma. I'm sure you'll find a few who are willing to help you, and for now, you're welcome to stay with us."

Ninka elbowed her hard in the ribs before he was even done talking. "Thank you, Majesty," Efa said, bowing so low her nose touched the water. She didn't know proper procedure for talking to the King of the Sea, but he seemed to enjoy it the further she went over the top. "It's an honor."

Without more than a nod, he swam off, and left them in the middle of a crowd of fascinated onlookers. Efa could feel her skin prickling. Ninka squeezed her arm and didn't even seem to mind - but of course she didn't, she knew all of these people. They weren't terrifying strangers to her.

"You did a good job," she said, her lips close to Efa's ear. "That went well."

"He seems to like you a lot," Efa whispered back. She had certainly not missed that kiss. "I didn't expect that."

"There's not many of us," Ninka said vaguely. "We all know each other."

"Were you..." She licked her lips. She wanted to say 'lovers,' but that wasn't a word that good selkie girls used, even if it was the truth of the matter. Where she was from people waited until they were married, or at least had the decency to keep it quiet and be ashamed of themselves if they didn't. (Bettan was one of those who tried to be discreet, who blushed and said it was wonderful and you can't tell anyone, not that there was anyone to tell. Efa had never been able to hate her for it.) Ninka didn't seem like the sort of person who waited for anything more than a passing whim.

Ninka looked away, her lips pressed together. "No, of course not. But his sister - you should meet her, anyway." She held out her arms and another fishwife swam over to them. "Efa, this is Afrit."

She looked more fragile than either Idain or Ninka, with long, almost translucent blonde hair and a thin smile. "Ninka and I have known each other for a very long time," she said. "And Idain is my older brother."

"So I suppose," Ninka said, laughing, "she's basically that princess you were hoping to meet earlier."

"It's great to meet you," Efa said. The other sirens were still staring, but they had backed off a little now that it was obvious Efa wasn't going anywhere. "Ninka, where's your family?"

She looked confused. "They're a ways off - they live with other people. There are more of them, but it's not as nice as Idain's kingdom is."

Efa looked more closely at the other people scattered around them. Some of them looked like they could be Ninka's relatives, but others were too pale and their jaws were shaped the wrong way. "So this isn't the town you grew up in?"

"It's not really a town," she corrected gently, and Afrit laughed. "But no, it's not. Idain decided to leave a few years ago, and some of us went with him. That's how he started his kingdom."

"She wanted to stay with me," Afrit explained, more than a little smug.

"I liked Idain, too." She put an arm around each of them, and they both leaned into the contact. "He's as wise as any king could be."

Efa shook her head. Their king - well, not their king, but the humans' king - was well-liked enough, as far as she could tell, but mostly the only things people said about him were gripes about taxes and jokes about countesses. But then Ninka was friends with her king's sister, which made her, while not a princess herself, certainly more of an important person than Efa had ever been.

"Welcome to the throng," Afrit said. She reached out and took Efa's hand in her own, squeezed it gently. "I know you'll have a good time."

"How did you meet?" Efa asked Ninka and Afrit. "Have you been friends your whole life?"

Afrit got a strange smile on her face, but one look from Ninka and it settled into a normal, toothier one. "No, we've only known each other a few years," she said.

They were on a sandbar hidden in the waters between two islands. Judging by the remains of a ship wrecked on its surface, and the delight with which Ninka had brought her here, Efa thought it might have been placed there specifically to trap up the unwary. The wreck was recent enough that the ship could still be identified and, indeed, entered, but not so recent that there was any evidence of its associated life. The islands on either side of the sandbar were close enough that Efa wanted to believe the men in the ship hadn't drowned. But then, they were small and sandy, unlikely to have fresh water, and perhaps that was a worse death.

"Idain decided he wanted to rule, so he joined my family's pod and took over," Ninka said. "Afrit just came along for the ride."

Afrit laughed. "It wasn't like that," she said. "We'd been alone so long - he raised me - and I was sixteen and he thought it would be good for us to have," she considered the right word, "people."

"A family," Efa said.

"No, we've always had plenty of family." Efa tried to imagine having just her brother, and that being enough. But then, Ninka had no family to speak of and she swore she was fine.

"The kingdom came later. He wasn't happy with the way things were run, and look! People came with us."

"How were things run in your old village?" Efa asked.

Ninka looked at her strangely. "They weren't. We did what we wanted."

Afrit said, "Idain brought order. Not like humans would, but he makes all the big decisions. And he put together trade agreements with the humans."

"So we can get the sparklies straightaway, and don't have to just pick at their leftovers," Ninka said, playing with a piece of gold she'd stuck through a small hole in her ear. People didn't believe in that where Efa was from. She wondered if Ninka had made the hole with her claws.

"What do sirens have to trade?" Efa asked.

They wouldn't look at her for a second, but then Ninka got her boldness back and winked. "Services."

When selkies threw a party, it was a warm, humble affair. There was usually an occasion - they didn't have many holidays, but they celebrated the change of the seasons as anyone would, they celebrated the birth of a child, the raising of a house, a wedding. The women would gather together and cook, where normally they just caught fish and ate them raw. They would cook soups and stews, and bake thick hearty bread to soak up the juices. They would roast fish on the fire, and clams and crabs in their shells, and serve them hot with herbed butter or fresh cream. The men would go to town and bring back beer so dense and sweet it could have been bread, spirits that everyone would pretend not to see until the party was well underway. And then the men, men Efa's father's age and older, would laugh and offer her a sip. She'd demur at first, but Bettan would say thanks, take the flask and chug, as though she needed any more fire in her blood. Efa would accept a drink, then, and for the rest of the night she'd be telling stories and kissing hands and faces. When selkies threw a party, they had a big fire on the beach, like humans did, and danced all night, which humans didn't.

A fishwife party was nothing like that.

Oh, there was food. The fishwives had collected a smorgasbord, fish gathered into a net and tied in the middle of the gathering. Anyone who was hungry could select a fish or - Efa witnessed this and then determined not to look too closely at the net, though she wasn't usually squeamish - carve a piece off of one and eat it. Lovers (she assumed they must be lovers) would slice off a piece of fish as a town girl would slice a piece of cake, or a roast, and feed them to each other, sharp claws brushing ragged teeth.

If Ninka had come to a party in Efa's village... probably the party would have ended. But if it hadn't, Efa would have stayed with her all night, introduced her to people, made sure she felt welcome. Ninka brought Efa in, split a fish with her, and then swam off to mingle so quickly that Efa didn't realize at first that she was gone. The party was held in a shallow, warm basin on the sea floor. For the most part, the fishwives gathered in small groups at whichever depths seemed to strike their fancy. Underwater, they spoke with their hands.

Above, though most of them could speak with Efa, with each other they used a language she'd never heard. She bobbed at the outskirts of their conversations and wondered if they'd come up with it themselves or borrowed it from humans. Selkies and humans spoke the same language, except that selkies had words humans did not know, and humans had words that selkies did not use. But there were a lot of ways that fishwives were not like selkies.

A hand took her by the shoulder and spun her around. She startled, then tried to relax when she saw that she was facing Idain. He was big in a way that Afrit wasn't, and though he was at least a decade older than Efa, he had a grin like a boy's. "I hope you feel welcome," he said.

Not at all. She shrugged awkwardly. "I didn't come to be welcome, Your Majesty."

He clapped her on the back and laughed. All of the sirens were more physical, she thought, with strangers than they ought to be. Selkies, and even the townspeople she knew, were very familiar with each other, but they had a right to be, when they were all related. Efa had a sense of Idain's interest in her much as she had a sense of Ninka's. Friendly, yes, and intriguing, but not something a good girl should get caught up in. "You're my sister's friend," he said, "so I expect that you will be, anyway."

She was trying to come up with the right thing to say - she'd heard that speaking to royalty was a struggle, that one had to be wary of both her words and of the king's, but she had never encountered it - when another man came up to them.

The first thing she noticed about him was that Idain perched almost imperceptibly higher out of the water when he approached. The second was that he had hair, dark as a selkie's, everywhere, and a grim look on his face, like even though he'd been invited to the party he didn't expect that enough of the fish would go to him. Unlike any of the other fishwives she'd seen, he wore armor, heavy metal braces over his wrists and a shining helm, in place of jewelry. It looked heavy enough to be a hindrance while swimming, though he had clearly developed the muscles to support it.

She noticed his arm last. It was at least as scarred as the rest of his body, even more so than Idain's, but the thing she noticed was that it was bent, as though it had been broken and never set properly. fishwives didn't seem to have real doctors. But then she remembered herself, and felt guilty for judging. There were two bones in the lower part of his arm, if he was built like she was - her mother had taught her that. If he had snapped them both, it would have been hard for any-one to set that break.

"Gefest," Idain said, "coming to meet our guest?"

Gefest examined her at least as carefully as she'd looked him over, his expression not quite friendly. "Everybody's talking about her," he said to Idain. And then Efa felt his at-tention shift to her, though he didn't move or change his gaze. "I've decided to help with your problem."

"That's so kind," Efa said, and took his hands in hers. "I can't thank you enough, I just know that-"

"I have an interest in such things," Gefest said. He didn't pull his hands away, but then neither did he smile.

"Still," Efa said, "no one in my village was willing to help, and everyone here has been wonderful."

Gefest wasn't at all interested in the praise, or at least wasn't willing to react, but Idain was bolstered by it. He patted Efa's back more gently this time. "My kingdom," he said, "is a lovely place, and my subjects give of themselves so generously."

Gefest pulled his hands away and stroked his beard. "I should be going," he said. "There are people expecting me. Idain." He nodded. "Miss." He squeezed her arm and then he swam away.

Efa blinked. "He's not much one for talking, is he, Majesty?"

Idain laughed. "The first thing you should know about sirens, dear," he said, "is that most of us are very testy. He's a good man, though. He keeps an eye on Ninka for me, and she's like a sister to me."

She believed that fishwives were temperamental - she knew Ninka, although only briefly. She wasn't sure that she believed in Gefest's goodness, but that didn't matter, because goodness was not what she wanted. Efa was a sweet girl, a responsible girl, a girl who did the right thing even when it was hard, and she knew that none of those things would get Bettan back. "His arm-" she said.

"Ah," Idain said, and clucked sadly, like a woman might. She wondered how often they held parties like this; he seemed to very much enjoy them. "Quite the tragedy. He suffers so bravely."

She wondered if Idain would have spoken so to Gefest's face. But then, she wouldn't have said anything where he could find out about it, either. "Was it a fight? A-" She didn't understand much of battles, of armies and strategies and all those things she knew happened sometimes. Where she was from, it was rare even that thieves or raiders became a problem. There was such bounty to be found in the sea that Efa imagined it would be easier for a man to feed his family off scraps than to abandon his dignity and steal from his neighbors. After all, any woman worth her wedding chest could make a measly soup from fish heads and bones, some tubers she'd sent the children to dig up. She could even get days-old bread from one of the taverns and it would soften in the broth. The violence in Efa's town wasn't the kind with marvelous armies and grand weapons. It was the kind where everyone knew something was wrong in the house of a man and his wife, so they spoke carefully with him and ignored her in the markets, because what was there to do that would make it better? Efa had never experienced real danger, the kind that they made into stories and songs, but surely it was worse than the sort she'd brushed against. Surely a bold man, one who'd survived battle, would see through the secrets and the impossibilities and pull them away as he would lift a maiden's veil from her face. "What I mean is, was he in a war?"

"Is there a war he hasn't been in?" Idain said. "He's not one for great battles - although I wouldn't want to face him in one - but he'll kill a man, or a dozen men, faster than you or I could spear a fish."

That was exactly what she needed. Why, a man like that, if she dragged him up onto the shore he could leap onto anyone who dared to hurt Bettan. "That's incredible," she said, and her horror was overwritten by her need.

"You'll find Ninka's that way, too," he said. "If it had worked - often I wish things had been different, and that she'd married my sister."

Efa paused. "I didn't think sirens married."

"We don't," he said, and he gave her an apologetic smile. "But you've met Afrit. She's always had me, she needs someone to protect her. I would feel better knowing that Ninka would always be that person."

Efa understood. She was that person for Bettan, or tried to be; Ninka almost was for Afrit, but couldn't seem to commit.

They spoke a while longer, until Afrit came over to check on them. She swam up from the side and kissed her brother on his cheek. Efa was suddenly very fond of her and glad that someone in this strange little kingdom acted normally.

"Did Ninka want you to check on me?" Efa asked.

"She's involved in a show of great strength," Afrit said somewhat dubiously, "so I thought she'd be fine by herself."

Efa smiled. "You wouldn't think siren parties would get rowdy, when you don't even have drinks."

"Sometimes we do," Idain said, "but we have to trade for them."

"And rum never lasts as long as you want it to," Afrit said. "Come on, let me show you around."

Afrit took her from group to group, and when she spoke to Efa in a language that Efa could actually understand, so did everyone else. The sirens were not the sort of people Efa would have approved of had she been home. As soon as Efa appeared (she suspected this, and Afrit confirmed it) they switched their conversation to tales of wicked doings. Their tempers flared unexpectedly, so that they would go from talking about normal things to hissing at each other before Efa could figure out what the offense had been. And their jokes, if they were jokes, were mean-spirited.

"Don't look," Afrit said when it was dark and they were traversing the space between groups, "but I think someone wants to see you."

Efa felt Ninka swim up to them more than she saw her, though the weak starlight reflected off her scales. Her hair was a mess, wet and rumpled, and all of her teeth were show-ing. "I won," she said, and kissed them both messily. "You should have seen."

"You won what?" Efa asked.

Ninka danced a little in the water, and took Efa's face in her hands, and flicked her tail, all of which Efa interpreted as a distraction while she decided whether she was going to lie. Efa wasn't naive. Not that there would have been anything wrong if she had been, with fishwives as they were.

"Some of us youngsters like to wrestle occasionally," she said. Efa blinked. "It's fun. I'm really good at it."

Efa wondered what 'young' meant to a siren. Ninka was a few years older than she was, which would have been young - though of age, and a full adult - in the selkie village. But she hadn't seen anyone older than fifty in Idain's kingdom.

"She doesn't like anything she's not good at," Afrit whispered.

Ninka put her hand over Afrit's face and pushed her deliberately under the surface. Afrit popped back up and spat a mouthful of seawater into her face. "I see I'm not wanted," she said, and swam away smiling.

"Shhh," Ninka said, but she didn't seem upset. She shimmied closer to Efa, put an elbow on each of Efa's shoulders, and watched her. Efa blushed, wished once again for some clothes. "Have you been having fun? Meeting people?"

Efa nodded. "I talked to a man who promised to help us. Gefest?"

"I was wondering if he would," Ninka said. "He gets bored."

"He must be a very valiant fighter, to still be so formidable with his injury."

Ninka let go of her and frowned. "His injury?"

"His-"

"No, I know," Ninka said. "It's - he doesn't like people talking about it. Not that it stops anyone."

"Oh," Efa said. "I'm sorry."

"But it's not a secret. It was like that when he was born."
She seemed to consider something, then added, "Just be careful. He doesn't like it when things get personal."

"So, it sounds like the problem isn't just that you don't
know where she is," Afrit said. They were sitting sprawled
out on a huge rock that protruded from the ocean and talking
strategy. Efa couldn't have been happier. Afrit had turned
out to be deadly smart and willing to help in the rescue effort.
Ninka, who was curious about the whole mess but also didn't
think herself of much use, deferred to Gefest. He was only
slightly friendlier away from Idain, but Efa couldn't complain
as long as he was willing to help.

"What do you mean?" Efa said. "Once I can get a hold of
her, we'll figure all the rest out."

"Not really," Gefest said.

Afrit nodded. "The problem is your 'sealskin.' If what
you're saying is true, finding that is what's going to be most
important."

Ninka said, "But it's going to be near her, isn't it?"

Efa covered her face with her arms and groaned. "Not necessarily," she said. "That's actually - I should have thought of
this. It used to be people would hide sealskins in the roof,
where they'd be hard to find, but everyone knows that trick
now. It'd be the first place she'd look."

"If it were me," Afrit said, sounding excited, "I'd keep it
somewhere she would never go, so she couldn't find it."

Ninka wiggled her tail, slapping it along the rock. It was hard for them to move up there. Efa wasn't even sure how they had all managed to pull themselves up at the same time, but apparently they did it often. "So she has to find her friend and the sealskin, too."

Afrit was sitting up, her tail curled neatly to her side. "Exactly!" She said.

"That, and retrieve them both," Gefest said. He looked Efa over skeptically. She was, in her human form, small even compared to other humans. She reached barely more than half the fishwives' length. Gefest could easily have squashed her in his massive hands. "I suppose you can't hold your own in a fight."

Efa blushed. She'd always had George or Rees or, in a pinch, Bettan to protect her. She wondered if she could get Rees to go in and save Bettan's sealskin for her, and then decided against it. He would probably be so mad at her for running away that he wouldn't even talk to her for months. "I've never really needed to."

"Stupid," he said.

"Don't be cruel," Afrit said. She was quiet and seemed frail, almost sickly, but her words held a lot of weight. Efa couldn't tell if it was because of her relative rank within the fishwife kingdom or because of her good sense. "I can't fight, either."

"You're the king's sister," Ninka said, laughing. "You can just sit back and let other people bedeck you with jewels and fish." The sirens didn't seem at all interested in clothing or most other human needs, but they loved jewelry. Ninka had a ring on every finger, and Afrit kept bright beaded strands twisted through her hair.

"I wasn't talking about Afrit," Gefest said, like a threat. "Her mistakes are her own." He was older than any of them, even older than Idain. He spoke like he was the adult and they needed to listen to him. "But you, Efa, should be ashamed of yourself."

"Why?" Ninka asked, her voice sharp. "She's not one of us. She lives in a pretty little town where things are safe. How could she ever have expected to need to know how to fight?"

He made a scoffing noise. "Obviously it wasn't that safe, or her friend wouldn't have been taken. You said you've always known this was a risk?"

Efa nodded, feeling small in nothing but her sealskin and her hair. (She had taken to braiding it and tucking the braid under itself in a desperate attempt to keep it from tangling, and while it looked better than the fishwives' it was still a mess.) "We're warned about it from the time we're children. I thought if I just hid my sealskin and was careful, everything would be okay. And no one seemed all that interested in me." That was a little bit of a lie. No one looked at her in the excited way they looked at Bettan, but men watched her with a contemplative eye, and if anything that scared her more. She couldn't stop thinking about how she could have been the one to have been taken, and she didn't know what felt worse, the fear or the sense that she was being disloyal. A true friend would have prayed that she could have been taken in Bettan's place. Her own terror wouldn't even have been a factor.

Afrit dragged herself over to Efa and gave her a hug. "It's going to be okay. You did the best you could."

Gefest sighed. "I don't mean to be harsh," he said, like the words cost him quite a bit. "I understand that you have a serious problem before you. But you're not going to succeed if you try to rescue her as you are now. You're no more prepared than a child."

Efa swallowed hard. That was exactly what she had been afraid of, what she had suspected this whole time. "Will you help me?" she asked.

"It'd be quite a challenge," he said. She couldn't tell if he meant for her or for him.

"I know. I'm not a fighter, but..." She thought of Bettan standing over an oven looking defeated. She'd known so many of those wives, women who were just so tired and couldn't think of anything to do but keep going on through every awful day. "I think I could learn."

Training with Gefest was one of the most difficult things she had ever done. He was twice her size and had fists like small boulders. In the water, he was unbeatable - and she didn't really think that was fair, when he was half fish and she had nothing but her scrawny human body to fight with. Not only could he duck all her blows, but he could swim around and get her from behind before she even realized what was happening. After the first time he grabbed her by the ankles and dragged her under, she started to feel a lot of empathy for those legendary sailors.

But that wasn't even the most humiliating part. The worst of it was that even when he dragged himself up on land, where he was a head shorter than her and had to pull himself about using his arms, he could still beat her nine times out of ten. Easily. By the end of each of their training sessions, she was left trembling and barely able to breathe. He swore he could see some improvement - "Not, mind you, that you're good enough to take anyone more than half-grown," - but she was starting to feel like it was hopeless.

"Are you sure we shouldn't just give up?" she asked one day while he was letting her take a break.

He laughed. She was both more and less frightened of him after spending a few days sparring with him. He didn't actually strike her as evil, but he was definitely ruthless, with the sort of cruel mind that would happily claw a man's eyeballs out. (He didn't let her actually practice that technique, but he assured her that it had worked well for him in the past, and if her claws weren't as impressive as his, well, "Scratch harder.") She knew him well enough, though, to get nervous when he laughed. It usually meant that he was about to get one up on her. "You want to save your friend, don't you?"

"More than anything," she said. She got up and went to sleep thinking about it. "But I don't think I'm ever going to be good enough to go in and fight my way to her."

"Then don't worry about that," he said. "That's not our goal, anyway. We just want you good enough in a fight that when you're looking for her sealskin and some guy grabs you, you survive."

She put her hands on her knees and looked up at him. "What do you think my chances are?"

He shrugged. "I'd say maybe half, unless he really wants you dead."

She groaned and they got back to work.

Over the time she spent working with him, she noticed something odd. A lot of the other sirens came to watch them. At first she thought it was just for humor, because she looked like an absolute disaster. But it tended to be the same people, and they weren't laughing. They just wanted to talk to Gefest, and even though he was generally opposed to letting Efa off easy he always gave her a break so he could talk quietly with them.

Maybe he was just being polite.

"I don't see why you're doing this," a woman told Gefest once, loudly enough that Efa could overhear.

"She's nice enough," he said, and that was the closest she had ever gotten to a compliment from him, so she treasured it. "She's just trying to help out her friend, it's not her fault."

The woman said something Efa didn't catch. "He shouldn't have let her stay, and you shouldn't be encouraging her. It's not natural."

Gefest came back to her from that conversation looking tired. "Sorry about that," he said.

After so much time spent learning to throw a punch, Efa felt brave. "What did she mean, it's not natural?"

He dug his fingers into his beard. "So you were listening," he said. She didn't deny it. "It's nothing. It's just that some of us think we shouldn't have humans around here. They cause enough trouble as it is."

"I'm not really human, though," she said.

"But you are, a little," he said, and they both looked down the long line of her legs.

She sat with the waves lapping at her feet, she crossed her ankles. "Do you think he'd kill me? The man who took Bettan?"

Gefest toyed with the brace over his arm, and Efa got the impression at once that he was fond of her and that he regretted it and that he regretted that she had asked. And that he would never touch her, in friendship or for other reasons, and her own relief at that was a shock. "I don't know him," he said, such a logical response that she knew it wasn't quite what he meant. "I think you're afraid of something else."

"What he'll do to her, is all," Efa said. "No man needs another wife."

"If it were about need, you wouldn't be so scared." He gestured for her to get up. "If you're fighting for your life, you'll be braver than if you're caught up wondering what he'll do once he catches you."

"I don't think people like me very much," Efa said the next time she and Ninka were alone together. Ninka had been taking off for days at a time while Efa strategized and learned to defend herself. Everyone swore it was perfectly normal, so

Efa tried not to be hurt. She always came back, which was the important thing, and when she came back they always slept close to each other.

"What're you talking about?" Ninka said, reaching down to scratch her scales. "I brought you, and Idain swore no one would bother you."

"Gefest said people think that humans shouldn't be around here." She licked her lips. "Humans like me."

Ninka cackled. "Of course people think you shouldn't be here, Efa. You worry too much. We're not like your happy little village where everyone plays nicely and listens to the council and likes each other." She had heard Efa's stories of her life back home, and on the whole she found them ridiculous. "Everyone disagrees, but that doesn't mean there's anything wrong."

"I just don't want to intrude."

Ninka grabbed Efa and pulled her close, watching her face. "Oh, wow, you're serious. Come on, everyone knows you're not really human."

"I can be, though."

Ninka rolled her eyes. She didn't tend to take anything seriously, Efa was starting to realize. "It's not the same thing at all."

"Even though there are selkies who can spend their whole lives with humans and never return to the sea?"

"Are they happy?"

Efa wasn't sure. She didn't think so, but everyone acted like it was possible. She didn't trust her own judgment in the face of conflict. "Maybe. I wouldn't be, but maybe."

"Then it's different," she said, and she was so firm about it Efa had to believe her. "Don't worry about riling up a few old fishwives, it's practically our job to get riled up. Just focus on finding your friend."

She couldn't think of anything else. She could hardly breathe with it sometimes. It was better, now, than it had been at first - time had made it less startling, and the feeling that she might find Bettan - but it still hurt. She didn't cry about it anymore, but she felt worn, like she had been stretched and now she couldn't go back to her original shape. She didn't smile as much. "I miss her so much," she said. "This is the longest we've ever gone without spending time together, by weeks."

"It's been, what, not quite a month?" Ninka said. She didn't have a very clear conception of the passage of time. Her entire life was made of choosing, simply because she wanted to, when to wander off and when to return home, without anyone to pester her if she spent too much time in either direction. She didn't need things like schedules.

Efa felt as though the days had been branded into her. "Soon, yeah. I'm scared I'll find her and she'll be totally different."

"She's your best friend," Ninka said. "How can she possibly change enough to ruin that?"

Efa could think of a few ways. Maybe Rees would be right and she'd have settled down into being a wife. Maybe she'd be glowing with the joy of a woman who had unpacked her wedding gifts and found beautiful embroidered linens. (Efa had always assumed that she would embroider all of Bettan's bridal things for her - not just waves, like her father would have made, but flowers, shining bedstraw in a squall.) Maybe she'd have turned stern-faced and pragmatic, like Efa herself, determined to get in the work no matter what had to be done, and no longer would she be Efa's escape from being a well-behaved young woman. Or maybe, if the marriage was worse than Efa dared fear, she would just go quiet and sad, or wistful and skittish. Maybe when they met again Bettan would be a married woman, with all of her newfound knowledge of what the world was like, and she wouldn't be willing to speak any of it to her childhood friend. "I don't know. Marriage changes people."

"And you're sure that she'd be married by now?"

"Well, there's no reason to wait," Efa said, bitter. "And there's hardly anything else anyone would want with her." At least, she hoped not. Of course there were things that someone could do with a beautiful, lively selkie woman who was all theirs, things that were worse than marriage, which at least everyone wanted. But if she thought that was an option she couldn't breathe, so she didn't consider it.

Ninka was just watching her, and for a second Efa wondered if maybe she shouldn't have snapped at her, if maybe she should apologize. "She means a lot to you," Ninka said, maybe placating.

Efa felt that was so obvious it wasn't worth saying. "She's everything," she said, "and she puts up with me. She likes me even when I want to stay at home and help out around the village."

"I like you even though you don't believe in fun," Ninka pointed out.

Efa blushed. "That's different," she said. "And I'm normally much more fun."

"I know. You're too busy now."

"Yeah."

Ninka ran her fingers through her hair. Everything she did to it seemed to make it messier. "I think I understand. Afrit and I were like that for a while."

"But you and Afrit..." Efa paused, tried to think how to word this. She felt like she was insulting them both just suggesting it. "You weren't exactly friends, were you?"

"I thought I already explained this to you."

She shook her head. Ninka had said quite a bit on the subject of her friend, most of it boundless praise like "She's a genius," and "Isn't she beautiful?" and "If anyone can help you figure out how to save your friend, it's her." And sometimes her words devolved into awkward, convoluted explanations of feelings and things that had happened and it only left Efa more confused.

"Oh," Ninka said. She pulled her fist to her mouth and chewed on her fingers thoughtfully. Efa tried not to wince at the sight of such sharp teeth pulling on her skin. "We were together, I guess you could say. Not like married - it wasn't that serious - but, um, we were pretty serious. I left my family and came here for her."

She left her family. "That's what marriage is," Efa said, her mind whirring. "It didn't work?" Failed marriages were common enough where she was from. They had to be, when so many relationships were founded on the theft of a sealskin.

"Like I said, it wasn't that serious. We were together for a few years, things changed, we're not any more."

She could believe, barely, that girls did that sort of thing together. She could even admit, in the part of her that brooked no nonsense, that there was something to the way she couldn't keep her eyes off Ninka's lips, couldn't look below the bare skin of her collarbone without turning red. But when she tried to think about it, even when she didn't put herself in the picture, there was just a blank. "What was it like?" she asked.

"Being with her?" She held her face in her hand, stroking the line of her jaw thoughtfully. "Intense. The first few months, neither of us wanted to do anything but be together. And afterwards, when you're that close to someone - I mean, people are always hard for me. But once you've got a girl, it's like swimming, you could do it all day."

"But what do you even do with a girl?"

"Whatever you want." The tone of her voice, low and amused, stopped Efa's every thought dead. "I'm sure you can think of a few things."

She couldn't. In fact, that was the problem, but she had too much dignity to admit it when Ninka seemed to think all people were born with an understanding of how to manage romantic encounters. "People don't do that where I'm from," she repeated.

"I'm sorry," Ninka said, not at all like she was making fun of her. "That's got to be confusing."

"A little," she admitted, trying to hedge. "I'm not sure what I think yet."

"There's time." But then she smiled, not as wild as usual but still a little mischievous. "It can be pretty fun, though, if you try it."

She was starting to get that impression. "Maybe," she said, "some time after I know Bettan's safe."

"Does Ninka leave like this a lot?" Efa asked on the third day of her friend's conspicuous absence.

She and Afrit were sprawled on a rocky outcropping by the shore. Afrit was braiding Efa's hair, a pursuit which frankly terrified Efa but which she allowed in the interest of interspecies diplomacy. "Hm," Afrit said. Her claws snagged in Efa's salt-tangled hair. At home, Efa brushed and oiled it regularly to keep it from being worn to tatters. A selkie girl's hair was her greatest extravagance, much as her sealskin was her pride. But here, it was bare to the elements, and she just had to hope that she wouldn't have to cut it and start over when she got home.

Afrit was clearly caught in her own thoughts. Efa cleared her throat.

"Oh. No, this is normal. She's more independent, maybe you've noticed."

Efa considered herself as independent as anyone needed. "So she'll come back."

"She always does." She carded her fingers through Efa's hair, and Efa gritted her teeth when it pulled. "She used to take me with her," she said, somehow more coy than usual. She looked so delicate, with her thin frame and translucent skin, that Efa wondered why she still got the impression that Afrit was playing at something. "We had a lot of fun together. But then she started leaving by herself again. That was when I knew it wasn't working."

"You're obviously still close," Efa said.

Afrit huffed a little sigh, and for a minute was too busy partitioning Efa's hair to speak. Then she leaned over to look Efa in the eyes, girl-to-girl. "She's stuck around a lot more now that you're here."

Efa's smile froze. "We're fond of each other," she said. And then, for clarity, "There's nothing happening."

"Of course there is." She sounded chipper.

"I don't want anything to do with your... lady."

Afrit gurgled and pulled the braid she had started making apart. She combed through Efa's hair once more, her claws gently scratching Efa's scalp. "My friend," she corrected. "That's all."

"I'm sorry," Gefest said one day when Efa had trained for hours and he was letting her catch her breath. "I haven't said so yet, and I should have. But I can't approve of you - of any-one letting themselves have that kind of weakness."

"I know," Efa said. In front of someone else, she would have cried. "I don't think it's possible to be angrier at your-self than I am for letting it happen."

But he was shaking his head. "You don't understand. To get her back you'll have to do awful things, and I like you, I think you mean well, but I don't think you've got it in you."

"I love her."

He reached out with his bad arm, and for a moment she thought he was going to touch her. Instead he pulled back, twisted his fingers in his hair and pulled it out of his face. There were scars everywhere, thin clean lines on his jaw and his hand, his wrist. "That's going to make it worse," he said, "when you can't help and the humans keep her forever. Even-tually you'll even stop being angry."

She considered that. "So, you think it's my fault?" She didn't know why she'd asked. He was going to say it was, and she was just going to have to be an adult and remember that it didn't change anything whose fault it was.

"No," he said finally. "What they did was wrong. I'm not surprised, but I think it was wrong. And anything you have to do to fix it-"

"It'll be the right thing to do," Efa agreed.

He laughed. "I don't think that matters anymore."

She leaned back onto her elbows, enjoying the sensation of the sand shifting beneath her. She had thought that she loved the water, that she could have spent her whole life in it and never minded, but being with the sirens had taught her differently. They never left, and Ninka admitted that she would have stayed in the deep if she could. Efa wanted shores and plants and to go into town and have a beer.

"Thank you," Efa said. She was surprised to discover that she meant it. She couldn't be angry at Gefest for not believing in her, not when she knew he wished that he could. And not when she couldn't, either, when she was only able to pull together the merest scraps of faith in herself because the alternative was unacceptable. "I'm trying to do, to be whatever she needs me to be. But I'm not sure how."

His teeth showed. She was always startled to see them. Gefest was so massive that that would have been enough. It was an embarrassment of riches that his body had also made itself sharp. "If I were a better man," he said, "I would tell you that that's no way to live, changing yourself for what's necessary."

"That's what my father would tell me," she agreed.

"But it's not a bad way to save your friend."

She bit her lip. "I wish you could come with me," she said. "You're a good friend, and you'd probably do a better job than I would."

"Not that good of a friend," he said, "and I don't go near humans anymore."

"But you did," she said hopefully.

He didn't say anything, like it wasn't worth justifying with a response, or like he wanted to let her down easy. When she thought for sure he wouldn't answer, he shook his head. "It's no secret. I was with a human once. It didn't end well."

"'With,'" she repeated.

"A blacksmith," he said.

Efa scrunched up her nose. "That's as human as you can get without being a miner," she said. And then frowned. "Are all sirens - do men always fall in love with other men?"

"A lot of us do," he said, "but she was a woman."

She was trying to understand. She didn't, but she was developing a sense of where her understanding would have been if she'd had it. "Ninka keeps saying-"

"That girl," he said, "adores you. Be careful what you do with it."

"How do you know?"

Gefest shrugged, his tail lashing the shore. "I know her. And she never even looks at anyone but Afrit."

She shouldn't have wanted it, it shouldn't have felt so normal, but it did. Efa had been a wanted child who had grown into a woman with a place in her family, a place in her village. "We don't do that sort of thing where I'm from," she said. He was looking at her like he had probably guessed that. "I don't think I've ever heard of - but if anyone had ever wanted to, I don't think they would have said anything. I'll probably still get married, no matter what happens."

He didn't seem surprised. "So, our Ninka?"

"I'd like to be her friend. I don't know what else."

"She's smart," he said, "and brave. I'm sure she'll be happy to help you."

It didn't seem fair, letting Ninka come and help her when Ninka obviously wanted more. She wondered what would be crueler, to bring her along and let the cards play out or to sneak away at the last minute and never say goodbye. She wondered if she could afford not to take any help that was offered. "What happened with your blacksmith?" she asked, suddenly curious. "Was that how-" She looked at the scars on his arm.

He went both cold and fascinated by what she had to say. "Was that?" he repeated.

And, well, she wasn't stupid. "Was there a fight?"

"No, nothing like that. Not that I haven't been in my share of scrapes, even a few for her." He leaned back on his arms, shifted his weight. "But humans, they can fall in love with people like us, they can fall in love with anything, but they can't really commit. I'm sure Ninka knows that already."

Ninka at her tenderest moments still had something cold and damp about her; she couldn't seem to muster the warmth that Efa had always assumed made up affection. Maybe it was what came of a life in the deep of the ocean, where there was no shelter. Efa knew the sea, too, knew it was relentless, that a man who fell in would have all the life of his body stripped from him. Ninka touched Efa's face with the soft undersides of her fingers, clammy but gentle, and Efa thought, she didn't know. That it was alien. That she didn't want it to stop.

"You're happy here, aren't you?" Ninka asked.

Efa nodded. Twilight was short where the fishwives lived. Only a little while ago it had been day. She took Ninka's hand from her face and spread it out on the surface of the water, feeling from the lines in her palm to the chitinous claws at the tips of her fingers.

Ninka didn't seem to mind. "I know you like me," she said. "And you seem to get on with my friends."

She didn't have many friends, so that was important. Efa sank in to her chin and looked up. It was, though it didn't occur to her, a trick she had learned from Bettan. "Do we have to talk?" she asked.

Ninka descended to her level, close enough that Efa could see the waves lap at her smile. "No," she said, "but you won't let me do anything else."

"Mmm." She frowned at the conundrum.

"Stay with me," Ninka said. "Stay here."

"I can't," Efa said. "I have things I need to do."

Efa could feel the water moving restlessly under the surface, spurred on by the churning of Ninka's tail. Ninka said, still pleading but now also firm, "It's not safe where you come from. I want you to stay here."

"It's not safe here!" Efa yelled. Then she heard herself, and lowered her voice. "I'm sorry. But your people destroy things, and I've seen their scars - Gefest looks like someone's tried to cut his arm off at least a dozen times."

Ninka put one hand on either side of Efa's neck, so that in the moonlight it was easy for Efa to look down the smooth, strong lines of her arms. "I don't look like I came through a war."

"Girls don't fight like boys do."

Ninka laughed. "I don't know what girls fight like," she said. "But when I get in a fight, I win, and I never let anyone touch me."

Efa frowned. She'd seen fights before - fist fights, and bar fights - but the most those ever resulted in was a bloody nose, a split lip, food splattered across the floor. And the men who fought were always apologetic in the morning, that they'd upset the women if not that they'd finally up and punched the bastard. She didn't think that was what it was like when fishwives lost their tempers. "Well, that's you."

"Don't you understand? If you stay here, you'll be safe from humans for the rest of your life. If you go back on land trying to look for her, I can't protect you anymore."

"It's not about me," Efa said.

"I think it is." Ninka took her arms back and crossed them over her chest. "You know, your problem is that you think you can be a human."

"I know exactly what I am."

"You think," she continued, "that when you're wearing your sealskin you're a seal, and when you take it off you can go walk into town and be a human, just because you look like one. But you're not. You're something completely different all the time."

"Your problem," Efa whispered - she felt wrong talking like that, "is that you think I can be safe if she's not."

"I'll protect you," Ninka said.

Efa wanted it so badly, and she shook her head. "She's my friend."

Efa woke first to a hand on her elbow. It was the middle of the night and someone was right next to her, making shushing sounds. "Huh?" she said. Last she remembered she and Ninka had decided to go to sleep.

"Hush," the man said. Gefest, she realized, and relaxed. After spending so much time letting him beat her bruised and exhausted, she trusted him implicitly. He was on one side of her, Ninka the other, and between the two of them she felt safe. "Ninka," he hissed, but didn't reach out to touch her. "Ninka, wake up."

Ninka was a deep sleeper. It took a few more tries before, her arms wrapped protectively around her body, she blinked heavily and started muttering to herself.

"There you go," Gefest said. "You've got to wake up, this is important."

Efa had expected that - had been hoping for it, in fact, and would have been furious if he'd gotten them up for no reason - but something about the way he said it jolted her the rest of the way awake. Important meant it wasn't like the times Bettan woke her so they could go swimming in the silent cold together. "What's going on?" she asked.

Ninka had her eyes open, mostly, but she kept closing them and nodding her head. Gefest looked to her and then back at Efa. "You two need to go."

"Mmkay," Ninka said. She snuggled back into the water.

They both watched her and shook their heads. "Go?" Efa said.

"Away from here, before anyone remembers you. Maybe for a while." He frowned, and she got the feeling that if she had been a human girl in a human town, she would have seen buildings burning in the distance. "Maybe you shouldn't ever come back."

She nodded, slowly making guesses at what had led to this. "Something bad happened, didn't it?" she said.

"Not exactly," he said. "But in the way you mean, yes. Things have changed."

She had goosebumps. Normally it was warm enough here that she could wear her human body to bed without getting the shivers, but she didn't normally wake up this late at night, either. "Is everyone okay?" she asked on impulse.

"It's too late to do anything," he said. He didn't sound as upset about it as he should have. "Just go."

That scared her. She wanted to scream and cry and demand that whatever had happened, he fix it right now. But she was a practical girl. She had never been one to lose her senses when there were things that needed to be done. "Do we need to be very quiet about this?"

"I think that might be best." Beside her, Ninka had settled back into quiet snores. Gefest took Efa's hand and squeezed it. "I've enjoyed teaching you. I hope you find your friend."

"Thanks," she said. And he swam away.

She got Ninka awake with a combination of cajoling, poking, prodding, and, finally, to their mutual displeasure, pinching the side of her arm so hard she expected Ninka to shriek. "Leave me alone," she said instead. She was made of stern stuff.

"I won't," said Efa, who was made sterner. "You've got to get up. I think we're in trouble."

She woke up enough to roll her eyes. "What makes you think that?"

Efa told her softly and in simple words. "He seemed like he knew what he was talking about."

By that point in her explanation, Ninka's eyes were wide. She muttered under her breath in a language Efa didn't speak. She had the decency to pretend not to swear in front of Efa, who had never had Bettan's skill at letting vulgar language roll off her like it was all a joke. She ended simply with, "That traitor." And then, "Afrit."

She was off almost before Efa could catch what she'd said. Afrit slept in the same place almost every night, by a mangrove island. Ninka swam along faster than Efa had ever seen her before, and Efa was only able to follow because she knew exactly where they were going. By the time Efa got there, Afrit had already been up for several minutes and Ninka was deep in explanation.

"I can't believe he would do that to us," Afrit said while Efa tried to catch her breath. She was trembling, her arms crossed. She reminded Efa of the porcelain dolls some of the town girls would handle so carefully. Maybe it was just the way Ninka looked at her. "He's our friend."

"We've got to go," Ninka said, low, urgent. Efa had never heard her talk like that before. "It sounds like there's been-" She grappled with the words, not sure of the right one. "A revolution."

Afrit nodded, her tiny, needle-like teeth biting into her lower lip. "As soon as we find Idain."

"We don't have time."

"Someone's got to warn him," she said.

"Darling," Ninka whispered, the word so tender like her heart was breaking, "you're the smartest person I know. They would have gone for him first."

Afrit took a deep breath, and then her face went completely still. Efa had always known she was a princess, but now she realized she was the type who gathered the troops and locked down the castle when it was besieged. "You don't have to accompany me, but I will find my brother."

Ninka swore again, but this time it was more resigned than angry. "You don't have to come," she told Efa. "At least one of us should escape."

Efa wanted to run. She knew it was the only smart move in this scenario. "No, it's okay," she said. "Idain - was kind to me. He showed me hospitality." Besides, Afrit positively glowed, and after all the time she had spent trying to find ways to save Bettan, Efa wanted to do what was right by her.

They took enough time for Efa to don her sealskin before they went off - she was a more graceful swimmer that way, and smaller. Even Afrit agreed that they needed to be stealthy. They set off, looking over their shoulders every few seconds, towards where Idain spent his nights. (Efa, raised on tales of kings and their battles, thought that perhaps it had been a terrible idea for the royal family to keep the same sleeping quarters every night. The sick feeling in her gut kept her from thinking too hard on it when she knew it was probably too late.)

They knew, really, that he was dead even before they arrived. But still Efa was surprised by the blood in the water. There was just so much of it, and part of her roiled to know that she was soaking in it. His body, skin torn in those curving slices, had fallen down towards the ocean floor. It took a moment for Efa to understand what had happened.

His head was gone, his neck open and pulpy. They had sawed through his throat with their claws.

Afrit rushed to the surface and screamed and screamed.

Ninka followed and held her, letting her hide her face. Afrit didn't rush to hold the body or kiss it goodbye. She couldn't even stand to look at it. And she couldn't stop screaming. "Hush," Ninka said, and "You've got to quiet down, they'll hear you," and "Please, baby, I know, I know, please." Efa had never heard her beg before. And still Afrit didn't stop. Whatever part of her was clear-minded and whole had died with her brother.

Efa bumped Ninka's tail hard with her nose. She couldn't talk to them like this, but with her whiskers she could feel things moving, and fast, through the water. Ninka didn't notice. She tried again, and then dove down into the seaweed. Closer, she realized with a lurch, to Idain's body.

She couldn't worry about that. They were coming.

Ninka saw them at the last possible minute and flinched away from Afrit, who only got louder when she saw what was coming. Someone grabbed Afrit. There was more blood in the water, his claws on her wrists.

Efa couldn't move. They didn't see her down low in the dark, not when Ninka's and Afrit's scales caught the moonlight so well. All her secret hopes that they would just want to talk were completely crushed. She couldn't stop watching as the man's claws cut Afrit from neck to nipple. Had their nails always been so sharp? Ninka's had touched her casually a dozen times without leaving so much as a scratch. She could barely think. Once she had seen a man on the street smack his wife, and that had left her shellshocked for days. She couldn't do this, but she wasn't brave enough to go and fight. She wasn't brave enough to sit and watch.

Just when she thought she was going to see her friends be torn apart, Ninka shrieked and lunged for the man holding Afrit. Her hand connected with his face and sliced it to the bone. He let go.

Afrit fled.

He would have followed her, maybe, or one of the others would have, but Ninka was a fury of teeth and talons. Gefest had never doubted her ability to fight - indeed, he stayed back now, out of her reach - but it hadn't occurred to Efa to wonder about it. She was so beautiful. Oh, mercy, there was so much blood.

That roused her just enough. She turned and left, chasing Afrit, trying not to feel like a traitor. Ninka was still back there, surrounded. But what could she do? She wasn't made to be a weapon.

Ninka caught up with them at dawn, her whole body an open wound and blood in her teeth. Efa was amazed that she was in a condition to outswim them - but then, their speed had dropped sharply after the adrenaline rush wore off. Afrit insisted on stopping every few minutes so that she could weep, and Efa had taken off her sealskin as soon as it seemed safe so that she could comfort her.

"You're safe," Afrit said when Ninka arrived, and burst into tears again. They embraced for so long that it made Efa lonely, but she tried not to take offense. (How many people had felt left out when she had taken Bettan's hand and skipped, singing, through town?) Instead she catalogued their injuries, which were gruesome, so dispassionately that she almost frightened herself. Afrit had the cuts on her wrists and arms from when she had tried to escape, and the parallel gashes on her chest. Those scared Efa the most, though they were only bleeding sluggishly. She couldn't stop thinking, *what a nasty scar those will leave, and, what will her husband think?*

But Ninka was a mess, she was well and truly wrecked. She had scratches everywhere, tiny nicks and long curving ones, big mottled bruises, and an especially jagged slice that ended just before her eye and made it hard for Efa to think. There was a circle of puncture wounds on her upper arm that, Efa realized with horror, had come from someone's teeth. Efa had never seen anyone so injured, not even that time that Rees had been helping to re-roof a house and the whole thing had come crashing down on him. She'd never imagined that someone could be hurt that bad because someone else did it to them.

Eventually Afrit's sobs weakened, and words formed from Ninka's incoherent reassurances. "Of course I got away," she said. "I wouldn't leave you guys. You'd get eaten without me."

"I thought we were all going to die," Afrit said, sniffling.

"Now you're being silly," Ninka said, though she looked like she had just barely thrown off death. "Efa was plotting her stealthy escape the whole time." She looked over her shoulder to Efa, and managed an uneven but determined smile. She must have hurt so badly. "I didn't even see you, did you leave before they got there?"

"No," Efa said. She was determined not to cry, but her voice was shaking a little. She paused to steady it. "I was watching."

"Ah." Efa expected her to start telling her off for not doing anything. "Smart. I figured if you thought we needed help, you'd swoop in and rescue us. I've seen those teeth of yours, even if most of the others haven't."

"What?" Efa squeaked. Her teeth? Sure, as a seal she had a powerful jaw, but that was for catching fish. She could hardly fathom turning it against another person.

Even if they were going to hurt her, or her friends? She thought of Idain's mangled neck and how helpless she had felt thinking she would have to watch that happen to Afrit. She didn't know.

"She came after me," Afrit said. "To make sure I was okay. Thank you so much."

"It's fine," Efa said. She swam over and patted Afrit's shoulder awkwardly. "Anything I can do to help."

Ninka disentangled herself from Afrit's grasp and looked them both over. "We need to rest for a little while. Where someone can't find us."

"I'm so tired," Afrit agreed. She stared down at her wrists like she couldn't believe they were hers. She seemed barely contained, like as soon as she had the energy she'd start screaming again.

"Come on," Ninka said. "I know just the place."

They ended up in the cave Ninka had shown her weeks before. Efa wasn't thrilled, but there wasn't any room to argue. It was secure and reasonably comfortable, big enough for all of them to hide out for a while.

The first few days passed quickly. Now that they were safe, Afrit was inconsolable, and everything but taking care of her fell away. Ninka, who normally only cared about the next adventure, was as gentle and patient as Efa had ever seen her. She spent hours holding Afrit, stroking her hair, listening to her babble so quickly Efa could barely keep up. They had long, shuddering conversations in languages Efa couldn't speak, and rather than being offended, she was relieved. Afrit kept trying to come up with logical explanations for how this had happened, intellectual reasons for why she felt so broken, and it was painful to watch her fail. There was no good explanation for this, no amount of thinking that would make it better. Efa kept coming back to it: they had sawed off his head with their claws, and she didn't even really understand why.

But she was starting to understand what Ninka and Afrit had been like, when they had been... together. Efa didn't believe in relationships outside of marriage. She believed that when people got close they set a date and made it official before the whole world.

But then there was Ninka's love for Afrit, so clear she could see it there in the dark of the cave. It was whole and warm and all-encompassing, the only thing strong enough to enfold her and keep her grief from pulling her down where she couldn't breathe. And Efa wanted to say that it was unnatural, that girls didn't do that, but sometimes she'd felt that way with Bettan. Like reaching for her was the only thing that steadied them both. She'd never wanted to kiss Bettan, of course, but she thought that maybe she understood if sometimes people felt that way.

She spent a lot of time thinking about it.

She spent a lot of time with Afrit, too, which surprised her. But Ninka at her absolute most patient could only hold her crying friend for a few hours before she got snippy and needed a break. She wanted to spend those breaks out and swimming around, but most of the time Efa was able to convince her that she needed to stay still and let her wounds heal. During that time Ninka sprawled out and fidgeted, sometimes silent and sometimes humming terrible songs she'd learned from human men. She was restless, but after the first few days Efa realized that she was terrified, too, and left her alone. It was her job to take care of Afrit.

They didn't cling to each other the way she and Ninka did, but they got on. Efa was patient and consistent, and she wasn't scared when Afrit howled with grief. People had always liked Bettan better, sure, but they trusted her, and she was glad for it. Afrit was quieter around her than she was with Ninka, more composed. Well, no wonder. Efa looked like a scared little human woman, maybe a young wife. Ninka was a warrior.

Afrit said things like, "Thank you so much for staying with me, I know it's not fun." And, "I can't believe it happened to him, he must have been so scared." She said, "You know, that was my only home. I thought I was safe there."

And Efa said, "I know, I know. I'm so sorry." And sometimes they just clasped each other's hands and held on while Afrit cried.

Efa got food for all of them, hunting in her sealskin and carrying fish back into the cave. Ninka wanted to fish, too, but she managed to open her wounds every time she left the cave to relieve herself, so Efa firmly rejected that idea. Afrit was comparatively easier to manage. She needed a lot of care, and probably wouldn't have done anything but collapsed and waited to die if she'd been on her own, but she didn't argue. She let Efa coax her into eating a few times a day, even if she took small bites and insisted she wasn't hungry. She wasn't like Ninka, who slapped her tail against the walls of the cave and complained.

And then, when it had been almost a week, Afrit left for an hour to swim by herself, and came back with her lips drawn tight. "We've got to do something," she said. Her tone was flat, dead, but maybe that was better than how raw it had been. "I can't spend the rest of my life hiding in a cave."

Ninka smiled for the first time in days. She said, "Well, miss, I've got a job for you finding a little lost selkie girl."

"I'll take it," she said. They still looked like they'd barely escaped death, but the cuts were starting to scab over.

{ 4 }

THEY LEFT THAT NIGHT BECAUSE THEY HAD TO GO SLOWLY AND THERE WASN'T ANY REASON TO WASTE TIME. Efa had expected that by the time she left the fishwives, she would be prepared to rescue Bettan. It hadn't worked out like that.

"You'll be fine," Ninka said during one of their breaks. They took them often so that Efa could look everyone (okay, mostly Ninka) over and make sure that there weren't any new injuries. "I mean, Gefest taught you how to fight before we had to leave."

"Before he betrayed my family," Afrit reminded them. Ninka was dealing with her feelings about Gefest by keeping them to herself, and Efa had come to the conclusion that there was nothing she could do but be grateful for what he'd taught her, but Afrit was still taking it pretty hard.

Efa said, "I'm worried he didn't teach me that well. Even he said I wasn't all that good."

"Then we can spar until you're more confident," Ninka said, like it was the obvious solution.

Efa just stared at her. She'd scratched most of the scabs on her arm off because they were too itchy. There was a healing wound on her cheek as long as Efa's middle finger.

"Okay," Ninka said, smiling, "so I don't look too good. But it's not like anyone's expecting you to land a punch."

By the time they'd been in the open ocean for a few days, both of the fishwives looked less like something a person would find in a butcher shop. All of Ninka's bruises, even the sickly yellow ones that were harder to spot under the brown of her skin, had faded, and her wounds stayed more or less closed. Afrit was in even better shape, although the cut on her chest had looked nasty and oozed pus for the first few days in the cave. They got to the place where Ninka swore she had met Efa relatively quickly, and it was no problem at all to just swim back in the direction she had come from.

At least, it was no problem until, shortly after they started, they hit land.

"Wow," Afrit said, staring at the expansive beach ahead of them, a small seaside village beside it. "Your home is really bright and sandy."

"I've never seen this place before in my life," Efa said. Not that that was hard; before Bettan's disappearance, she'd never left home except to go to the human village. She'd never been so far inland that she couldn't taste the sea. "We're lost."

"No problem," Ninka said, grinning like she was delighted to have a chance to show off. She probably was, too. "I'll just go talk to some boy on the docks over there and get him to give me directions."

Efa and Afrit looked at each other for a long moment. Afrit was the one who spoke. "It's not that you're not beautiful, of course," she said.

"What?"

Efa looked her over. She did that a lot. The sight of her didn't make Efa feel scared anymore, like it had the first few days after the fight, but she was still impressive to behold. It wouldn't have been possible, not anywhere, for Efa to put her palm down on Ninka's skin without touching a healing wound.

Afrit's gaze was more of an inspection. She said bluntly, "I think if you go up to some poor man now, he'll die of fright. I'll do it."

"No," Ninka and Efa said at the same time. Afrit was fragile; they were both protective of her. Efa continued, "It's fine. I should be the one asking anyway, I know where we're headed."

It wasn't until a few minutes later, when they got close enough to shore that they could pick out the forms of individual humans, that she remembered she hadn't brought any clothes with her. She had gotten used to being among the sirens, who mostly wore no clothes and either didn't notice or didn't care if she was bare except for her sealskin. "Oh no, I'm naked," she said.

"I noticed," said Ninka.

Afrit frowned. "Humans have a problem with that, don't they?"

"A little," she said. But it couldn't be helped. And maybe they wouldn't mind her. The oldest stories about selkies, the ones George told her sometimes from before humans ever even knew what they were, were about beautiful women dancing naked on the beach. Efa didn't think of herself as beautiful, not the way Bettan or Ninka were, but she knew that just by being a selkie she made boys see her as exotic. "Could you take my sealskin?" she asked Ninka, holding it out.

"Are you sure?" Since Efa had explained what it meant, Ninka hadn't so much as glanced at her sealskin, and Afrit had been so similarly solicitous that Efa thought they had probably had a talk at some point. Even when they touched Efa, they stayed far away from the sealskin she held close.

"I don't want someone to grab it. I don't know how much these people know about selkies," she said. She couldn't say what would be worse, to have her sealskin snatched because someone didn't realize it was important to her, or to have it stolen because someone was especially fond of her and wanted to keep her around. She had been protective of her sealskin all her life, but now she was especially determined not to take chances.

Ninka took it and folded it over her arm. "It's so soft," she said, smoothing it down.

Efa flushed. "That's my skin," she said. "Don't get weird."

"Are you going to be okay?" Afrit asked. "We can come with you or something."

"You look like a pair of monsters from the deep," Efa said, grinning. "It'll be fine. I'll be right back just as soon as I can find someone who knows where we're headed."

It was hot on the beach, which was just more evidence that they were in the wrong place. It never got so warm back home that there wasn't a cool breeze, and it had been coming up on winter when she'd left. She appreciated it now, though, when she had no clothing and was on shore for the first time in ages.

By the time she got to the first of the buildings, the ends of her hair had dried and were starting to curl. She stood tall and walked, casually as she could, past a cluster of teenage boys. They were staring, which meant that they wouldn't be any help.

They muttered at each other as she got up close to them, but she couldn't understand what they were saying. One spoke, then another, and she caught half of it, *she* something. Then they all laughed. Efa watched the ground. The streets here were made of loosely packed sand, and the roofs of the buildings were flat. She missed her home, and people speaking in languages she was comfortable with. She was used to talking with Ninka and the other fishwives in trade-tongue, but it wasn't the way she thought. Before this trip, foreign languages had only ever been a game to her, something she and Bettan picked up and practiced together because they liked to make all sorts of friends.

She was trying very hard not to be afraid of the boys. They were young, all four or five of them, not a one older than sixteen. They looked like children to her. Selkie pups the same age gathered into troupes and roamed.

But selkie boys didn't care if she was naked. And she understood their language. And they knew that if they so much as looked at her the wrong way, Rees would beat them so hard that next winter they'd still struggle to walk.

One of the boys shouted, and he was definitely talking to her. After a few seconds, the words made sense in her mind. "Hey, what's your name?"

She kept walking. They followed, still trying to get her attention.

This wasn't exactly the first time this had happened to her. Even at the Hungry Hogfish, things got rowdy sometimes, and they always had to walk past a few other bars in order to get back home from town. Usually Efa hunched her shoulders and Bettan shouted back. Now Efa was thinking about Gefest and how yes, he had been right, it had been stupid of her to go her whole life assuming everything would be safe. Now here she was trying to decide if it would be better to keep walking or to turn around and face them.

Ahead of them all, a woman stepped out of a shop and looked them over. She was a little older than Efa's mother. Her graying hair was pinned up and covered with a shawl, and she carried a few loaves of bread. Her mouth fell open when she saw Efa. Then she shook herself off like a dog. "What are you boys doing?" she asked. Her voice was loud and firm, and a dozen times easier to understand than the boys'.

One of the boys tried to defend himself in an increasingly high-pitched voice. Efa couldn't understand what he was saying. The woman walked over and put an arm around her. She sagged with relief, and stood there watching while the woman dressed the boys down. They left as quickly as they could, turning down the street and out of sight.

Then the woman smiled at her. "Are you okay?"

"Uh, yes," Efa said. So far, so good.

"You're not-" And something she didn't understand.

"I don't speak," she tried, "good."

"Oh." The woman hummed to herself and repeated what she'd said before, but this time she tugged at her blouse. One of those words meant clothes, probably.

She tried to come up with an explanation for her nakedness that would make sense. She didn't know the word for selkie, though, or seal. "I'm not-" she said, but then she realized she didn't know human either. "I don't have any clothes."

"Are you okay?" the woman asked again. "Are you-" and that had to be hurt.

"No, no. I'm good." She tried her most reassuring smile, something that would dispel all those fears this woman had about why a girl might end up naked in the streets. "I am, I want to go home."

The woman nodded and slowly unwrapped her shawl, put it over Efa's shoulders. Efa took it and covered herself. Then the woman guided her down the streets. That wasn't exactly what she'd meant - she needed to go to her own home, the little island where she and her parents and Rees and Bettan lived - but she was too busy being relieved to argue.

Soon they arrived at a small house. "Here we are," the woman said. And then, smiling, "My name is Vera."

"It's Efa," she said, and fiddled with the shawl.

Vera let her into the house and gestured for her to seat herself at the kitchen table, then disappeared into another room. She came back with a pink dress about the right size, saying something about her daughter.

"Thank you," Efa said, and changed into it quickly.

Vera looked her over and nodded, a warm smile on her face. "Did you eat?"

"No," Efa said, "but-"

She wouldn't listen to any of her complaints, or to anything at all, until she'd stuffed three buns filled with spiced meat into Efa's belly. Food back home tended toward fish of all sorts, but this was good, too. Efa thanked her throughout the meal, and again when she was done. Maybe she was a barbarian who walked through the streets naked, but at least she was going to be polite.

"It's nothing," Vera said. Efa hoped she was telling the truth, that she wasn't going to have to miss dinner that night because she'd given it to a girl who could have caught her own. She had to repeat her next words before Efa caught all of them - "Can I help you?"

"I'm lost," she said slowly. "I need to go home."

"Where-" But Efa understood none of the rest of her sentence. And when she named her village, Vera frowned. "I don't know." She didn't know the human town, either, or any of the cities further inland. It was only when Efa named her kingdom that she nodded and said, "Ah! It's north of here. I can show you the road to take."

"The road," Efa repeated weakly.

"And who to ask at the next town." Then she muttered to herself, something about "...if you can't. But I'll write you a letter."

"Thank you," Efa said. She took a deep breath so she could try and get the words in the right order. "But I don't need that. I can swim."

Vera gawked. "All that way?"

"Yes, ma'am."

She leaned back in her chair and thought for a moment. When she spoke, her voice was soft. "You look like a normal girl, but you're not." She didn't sound offended, not exactly, but Efa still felt like she had disappointed her. Like she had meant to offer hospitality to a sweet girl in a tight spot, but instead had been tricked.

"Not exactly," she said. "But I only want to go home, to my family. I'm not normal, but I'm not a monster."

She couldn't tell if Vera believed her. She looked quietly troubled, but that might have been because she wasn't happy with what she heard. And there was her lack of humanity, which Efa knew cast doubt on everything she said or did. A human girl who walked about naked could only be a victim, at the very least of a very cruel practical joke. But some strange monster woman could likely take care of herself, and might even be dangerous. Efa tried to adjust her hair so that it was a little less wild, and sat with her ankles crossed. Vera said, "You don't look like a-" and then it took her a moment to just listen to the last word and hear siren in it.

She could barely believe that Vera knew what fishwives were. Back home they were a silly legend, half-fish girls who destroyed whatever they felt like. "I'm not a siren," she said. "I'm a little like them, but more friendly."

Vera laughed. "You do seem like a nice girl," she said. Efa felt herself relax, although she was still sitting up as tall as she could. "Do you need to spend the night?"

"No, thanks. I just needed to know where to go."

She nodded. "North will get you there."

Efa escaped an hour later with Vera's blessings, the dress, and a rag with half a dozen pastries wrapped up in it. Ninka and Afrit were sprawled out in the surf, catching some sun and letting the water wash over them.

"You look pretty," Ninka said.

"See, I told you she'd make out great," Afrit said, pushing herself up onto her elbows. "That's way more than just directions."

"I met a lady," Efa explained. She sat down on the damp sand, mournful for her dress. It was just plain cotton, but it was well-made, and with all the abuse she put her dresses through she was always on the lookout for new ones. "Can you guys eat people food? She gave me a bunch."

"We're people, too," said Afrit.

Ninka laughed at Efa's stunned expression. "You see me eat bones every day, and you're scared there's anything this body can't handle?"

Efa blinked. "I don't think I could handle bones in this body."

"We're built different," Ninka agreed. "I never say 'no' to perfectly good food. Hand it over."

She did, and they made quick work of the food. They couldn't bring any of it with them. Ninka gobbled a meat pie bigger than Efa's fist in two bites. Afrit split a sturdy fruit pastry down the middle and handed the other half to Efa. It was all a little overwhelming for Efa to watch. She had wished for an army to help her rescue Bettan, and well, they certainly ate like one. The three of them got crumbs everywhere, and Ninka laughed and laughed.

It felt like ages later that they arrived on an island Efa recognized, just a short swim away from her home. It was cold, and the shore was rocky, and when Efa slipped off her sealskin and said "We've made it," both Ninka and Afrit looked disappointed.

"Well," Afrit said, crossing her arms over her body, "I guess it could have been colder."

"Maybe if we showed up in the middle of a snowstorm," Ninka said. She had never seen snow before, and as far as Efa could tell she was torn between thinking it was a lie made up to mess with her and thinking it was proof that a land was utterly inhospitable.

"It hardly ever snows here," Efa promised them. "And it's not even that bad out yet. This is balmy for this time of year."

They both looked at her with such lost, betrayed eyes that she was reminded of a gull chased off with rocks. "It gets worse?" Afrit whispered.

"There are ways to keep warm." They stared at her, solemn and covered in goosebumps. Efa realized that in her experience, most of those ways boiled down to 'wear your sealskin and huddle for warmth.' She frowned. "Look, give me a chance to go home and tell my family I'm alive, I'll get right back here and start you a fire."

They considered this for a moment. "You could start us a fire and then go, once we're warm," Ninka suggested. She gave a winning smile like that would make her argument more persuasive.

"I don't have flint here," she said, and shrugged. "I have to go get it first."

"You don't want us to come with you?" said Afrit.

Efa tried to imagine what would happen if the people of her village stumbled upon two fishwives living among them. They would scream, and then - well, they wouldn't try to kill them. No selkie had done battle with anything more frightening than an albacore in at least two centuries. That was her whole problem. So they probably wouldn't pick up weapons they didn't have, they would just scream.

And, worst of all, Rees would sigh at her and talk about what this means for our family. Like the most important thing was his reputation and it was her duty to safeguard it.

"I don't think it's a very good idea for you to meet them," she said. "They might not take it well."

"Are your people afraid of sirens?" Afrit asked, like there was no reason they would be.

Efa looked at them and catalogued their bodies once again; it had become habit. Teeth, claws, piercing eyes. "Yes," she said. "They definitely would be."

"You're not," Ninka said.

"I'm terrified," Efa said, smiling. "'Cept you sang to me until I forgot how it felt."

She got back to her house and changed into a dress without anyone noticing her. No one had moved any of her stuff, which was both a relief and a surprise - had they even noticed that she was gone?

She went looking for Rees, who was brooding, as usual. He saw her and stood to fling his arms around her. For a moment they held each other so tightly that she thought she might pop. Then he let go just a little. "Don't ever do that again," he said. "Mom and Dad thought you'd died for sure."

"And you didn't?" she said, a little choked up. She blinked hard, swallowed.

"I figured you'd done something stupid, like go looking for her yourself." He adjusted his arms a little, held her head against his chest.

"No, I just-" She couldn't tell him the truth. It hadn't ever been like that before. When they were children together, she'd been able to tell him anything and know that he'd help her keep it from their parents. Now that they were grown, her parents wouldn't try to stop her from doing things, but Rees would. "I just couldn't stand to be here. I needed some time."

"You could have talked to me," he said, and he sounded so sincere that she regretted leaving without him. "I miss her, too. It's been hard, with both of you gone. Everything all quiet."

"Oh," she said. She hadn't thought of that. "I'm so sorry."

"It's fine." He let go of her and sat back down, patting the space beside him. She sat.

"Does that mean she's still missing?" she asked.

He nodded. "It looks like you were right. She's probably married with kids by now." She couldn't imagine either of those. "Are you going to stay, at least?"

"Yeah, I think so. For a while."

He looked so tired, like responsibility was crushing him. Like it had killed him a little to have her gone. She wanted to tell him to relax. "You're still going to look for her," he guessed.

She smiled tightly. "I can't not."

"I understand," he said, and she wondered if he did. "If you can get her back, I'm not going to stop you."

It was better than she had expected of him. "Do you think I can?"

Rees looked at her for a long moment. Then he leaned back onto his hands. "I think these sorts of quests probably happen all the time, and the reason you don't hear about them is that they hardly ever succeed."

She had to try not to be mad, or hurt. "But she's my best friend."

"Efa, you can't possibly think that you're going to do better just because you love her more."

"Why not?"

She knew she sounded childish. He frowned and took in a big breath of air, then let it out slowly and closed his eyes. "Because that's not how it works," he said. "Just wanting a thing doesn't make it happen."

She knew that. Truly she did. But she couldn't help believing that maybe, if she wanted something so badly she couldn't breathe a breath of wanting something else, that would help her find it. And she wanted Bettan back like that, so that she would easily have forgone pretty dresses and food and rest. "I have to try," she said.

"Yeah," he said. "I suppose you do."

They sat in silence for a while and she relaxed. She had missed him. "Hey," she said eventually.

"Hmm?"

"Could I borrow your flint?"

He opened his eyes. "You want to start a fire."

She made eye contact and smiled. "Yes."

"You're not going to burn down the town, are you? That won't get her back."

"Of course not," she said. "I just want to be able to build a fire, and I don't have my own supplies."

She thought he believed her pretty much not at all. "You promise you won't do anything crazy?"

"Swear on my life," she said.

"It's in my house, you can find it yourself. But one more thing."

"Anything."

"Go talk to Mom first," he said, clapping her on the shoulder. "She'll need to see you to believe you're okay."

It was a good thing that she had a long swim to the island where they were staying after she saw her parents, because she needed some space to decompress. She wasn't sure if she was guiltier because she had terrified her parents by leaving or because she still hadn't rescued Bettan. It had been so long since she'd left, and she couldn't believe that she hadn't come up with something yet.

I'm doing my best, she told herself, and tried to believe it. She swam a little faster. Ninka and Afrit were probably turning blue.

Her mother hadn't cried, but she suspected that was only because her mother was a very put-together woman. And because they'd met as seals, who weren't as prone to hysterics as humans. Mom had said, "Oh, Efa," and Dad had said, "You could have died out there and we'd never have known." And her parents didn't talk to her like she was a child much anymore, but it still killed her to know that she had disappointed them.

The sun went down as she swam. Ninka and Afrit were huddled against a rock and making sad noises to each other when she showed up. "You're back," Afrit said.

"We thought we might die," Ninka said piteously. It was hard to believe that she'd fought off a crowd of murderous sirens with her bare hands and teeth.

"I just had to check in with my family," she assured them, folding her sealskin up. She put it on the ground and sat her bag down on top of it.

"Are they happy to see you?" Ninka asked. She acted like she didn't understand the idea of families, but she knew well enough that Efa's was important to her.

"They're delighted to see me," she said, sighing. "I thought they were going to kill me, they were so angry."

Ninka frowned. "But you came back."

"I don't think they wanted me to leave in the first place," Efa said.

Afrit coughed delicately. "I think I remember hearing something about a fire?"

It took her a few minutes for her to get the tinder going, and longer for her fire to turn into a respectable blaze. Once it had, the fishwives settled alongside it, curled up and rubbing their arms for warmth. She thought it was nice, too, but unlike her companions, she didn't need to sit so close she blistered.

"Thank you," Afrit said when she stopped shaking. "I don't know how we're going to survive here if we can't handle the cold."

"You'll get used to it," Efa said. She wasn't completely sure. "It's not so bad."

"If I lived in a place like this," Ninka said, "I'd move."

Efa sighed. She was starting to get a sense that there were reasons why no one she knew had ever seen fishwives before. "I happen to like it here," she said.

They all stared into the fire, and soon Afrit fell asleep. Efa planned. Tomorrow she would start her search in earnest, and soon Bettan would be back with her. She wasn't completely sure what would happen after that - would the fishwives go back home, or would they stay with her and risk freezing to death? Would Bettan even want to stay friends with someone who had taken so long to rescue her?

Not that it mattered. She had to go through with it. It seemed reasonable that Bettan might not forgive her; she was angry enough at herself.

"Hey." Ninka had come to sit by her, so that they were both on the opposite side of the fire from Afrit, and she hadn't even noticed.

"Hi," she said. "You're not asleep yet, either?"

"Not on land," she said, making a face. "I'll probably freeze to death in the water, but at least I'll have the waves to rock my cold dead body."

Efa laughed. "You're not that bad," she said, touching Ninka's arm with the backs of her fingers. "The fire's got you all toasty."

Ninka shivered vigorously, but she was smiling. "It's seeped into my bones, though."

Efa wiggled closer. "We'll have to protect you from the nasty weather," she said.

"You will." She bumped her arm up against Efa's. "You're why I'm in this awful place."

She could hear the fire crackling, waves hitting the rocks, wind cutting through the trees. She looked across the fire long enough to be sure that Afrit was definitely asleep. (Her mouth was open, and there was drool leaking out of it.) Then she leaned in and kissed Ninka, and pulled back so quickly that she almost wasn't sure she'd really done it.

Ninka's face stayed absolutely still. "I thought girls don't do that sort of thing," she said.

"Well, obviously you do."

"I do," she agreed. She sounded so smug that Efa wanted to punch her. But then she pulled Efa towards her, one hand on Efa's hip and the other in her hair, and they were kissing, and Efa decided that a little confidence could probably be excused.

Her teeth were sharp and her hands insistent, but she was so gentle that after the first few seconds Efa stopped worrying. Ninka certainly seemed to know what she was doing, and Efa was willing to go along with that. She was going to have to apologize for every time she'd made fun of sailors entranced by fishwives' beauty, for every time she'd told told Bettan that it just wasn't possible to lose track of what was happening and accidentally get into trouble.

Oh, no. What was she doing?

"Mmm," she said into Ninka's mouth, "wait."

Ninka made a little disappointed noise, twisting Efa up in all sorts of ways she couldn't think about, and pulled away. "Yes?" She bit her lip, waiting, and Efa had to close her eyes to speak.

"I shouldn't be doing this," she said. "I have important things to worry about. I mean, it's not that I don't want to. But Bettan's out there and I can't believe I'd let myself just forget."

Ninka listened to the whole speech patiently. "You're not betraying her by doing something else for a few hours. It's not even like you could be looking for her right now, it's too late."

"A few hours," Efa repeated faintly.

"I'm optimistic." They looked at each other for a moment. Ninka brushed Efa's hair behind her ear. "Look, it's your decision what you want to do, but I can't keep doing this thing we've got right now. I won't."

"This thing?"

She pursed her lips and took a moment to come up with a way to say it. "The one where you keep kissing me and changing your mind. You get some leeway because you're new, but usually you have to decide before you bring someone else into it. It's just good manners."

"I didn't know you were all that into etiquette," Efa said to cover her embarrassment.

"Sometimes I take an interest." She was barely lit by the fire, and she was so beautiful Efa didn't know how she'd ever thought she wanted boys. "I'll be fine either way, but you've got to figure out if you like me."

"I like you," she said without thinking. "A lot."

Ninka had been acting like she didn't care for the whole conversation, but now her face lit up, not soft but warm. "That's a good start," she said. "We can work from there."

"I can't stop thinking about - the thing with Bettan," Efa said. For weeks there had been nothing else in her life. She was breathing it, she was full with it, it was making her sick. She could feel her fear and her anger and her guilt buzzing around inside of her where once she had been quiet. She would never have dared say that she was suffering, not like Bettan was, but she wasn't well, either. Bettan was gone, and she couldn't put that down long enough to rest. "It's driving me crazy."

"Sweetheart," Ninka said, and she was so tender that Efa just ached to her tips. "The only person I've ever loved, her brother dies, just like that, and now we can't go back to the only place I've ever loved. And you think I don't know that sometimes things come along and swallow up your whole world?"

"Oh." She swallowed and slouched forward, and when Ninka put an arm around her she let all of her weight fall on Ninka's ribs. "I'm just so tired. It never goes away."

"I know," Ninka said. But it wasn't quite sympathy, and Efa thought of Gefest, thinking he'd never want her and what a relief it had been. She wasn't relieved now, just embarrassed.

George was so excited to see her that when she arrived at the Hungry Hogfish he immediately got up and found her a table himself. He sat down right across from her and called to Mary to bring her a drink and some food. "I've got money right here," she insisted, but he waved her away.

"We're not doing so badly I can't afford to give you something on the house," he said. And then, hopeful, "You find her?"

She shook her head. "I'm still looking, though. Have you heard anything?"

"Not a whisper," he said. "It's like this man vanished."

Efa frowned. She was still hoping that Bettan's kidnapper was from around town, that at the very worst he'd gone further inland. She didn't know how she'd get Bettan back if he'd stowed away on a ship and headed off to a faraway island. "Well, if you hear anything, let me know," she said, disappointed.

He promised, and left her to contemplate her problem over a meal. She was confident that if she could just find Bettan, all the rest would be a cinch. She had years of getting into trouble behind her. She had Ninka and Afrit's support. And between Gefest and Ninka, she knew how to throw a punch - or, more to the point, duck one. A million times she had envisioned the sneaking around, the strategy, the rough-and-tumble fights she would go through to save Bettan. But she wasn't a tracker. She didn't know how to find someone who wanted to be found, much less someone who was being hidden.

She finished her ale and picked at the remains of her food, too far gone to be hungry. She hardly noticed when Mary came over to clear away her dishes, or even when she tapped her lightly on the shoulder.

"Efa?" Mary said, and she looked up. Mary was, like many of the married women Efa knew, quiet to the point of demurring to everyone. Efa didn't think they'd ever had a real conversation, not beyond 'Would you like some more ale, miss?'

She tried to shake off her mood and at least pretend to be friendly. "Yes?"

"George told me what happened to your friend."

Efa's face froze in a tight smile. She did not feel like listening to strangers' sympathies. "Thank you, it's very hard."

Mary made a face and tried again. "There's someone that I think you should meet."

Efa brought her voice down to a whisper. "You know someone who can tell me where she is?"

"Not exactly." She looked a little hurt, like this wasn't going the way she had hoped. "I know someone who I think can help. Will you trust me?"

She didn't have much choice. She agreed, and Mary led her through the back door and into the courtyard that opened up on George's house. Efa had known that it was

there, of course, but she'd never actually been through this
way. George's house was of a good size, as befitted a respectable businessman with a large family, and was well kept up.
Mary took her into the kitchen and sat her down at the table.

"Just a moment," she said. Then she stepped into another
room and called, "Nellie! I need you in here!"

Efa could hear someone else - presumably Nellie - walk
down the stairs and over to Mary. "I just put the baby down,"
she said. She sounded firm, no-nonsense.

"Sorry," Mary said, suddenly warm. "How is he?"

"He's great," said Nellie, "keeps trying to pull my hair.
What can I do?"

"I brought you Efa. The-"

"Friend of that selkie girl Dad keeps talking about?" Nellie
finished. "The one who got taken?"

"I thought you could help her. I thought you'd like to."

It was quiet for a moment. Efa crossed her ankles and
fidgeted with a bit of trim that was falling off her dress.

"You know, you're not supposed to know any of this," Nellie said. Efa had to strain to hear her.

There was a smile in Mary's voice. "I may not be your
mother, but I am a mother," she said. "I know what you children get up to."

They walked back into the kitchen. Nellie was a tall young
woman in a rough gown, with darker hair and eyes than
George's. Efa thought she would have been attractive if not
for the way she held herself, more like a lanky youth than a

lady. "I'm Nellie," she said, nodding. "Mary says we might get along."

Mary looked over the two of them with the expression of one who thought that she had perhaps gotten into more than she had expected. "I've got to get back to work," she said. "I'm sure Nellie will take just great care of you."

After she left, Nellie sat down at the table with Efa. "So, what did she tell you?"

"Nothing," Efa said. "Just that she thought you might be able to help me get Bettan - my friend - back."

Nellie groaned loudly and covered her face with her hand. "I can't make you any promises. But we can try."

"We?"

"Have you ever heard of the Daughters of the Sea?" That was how she said it, like the words themselves were important.

Efa shook her head.

"Good, because we're supposed to be a secret organization. For now, anyway." She smiled, and there was something about it that made Efa feel nervous and excited at the same time. "Pretty soon, mark my words, we're going to run this town."

They met an hour after the sun set at the edge of town and crowded into a little rowboat. Nellie greeted Efa with a nod and introduced her quietly to the rest. Clara was a small girl with a high voice who was younger than all the rest of them. Louise dressed like a fisherman, in pants, and with her hair pinned up tight to her head. Efa mistook her for a boy at first, and spent the first twenty minutes apologizing over and over again. And then there was Jesse, who really was a boy.

"I thought you were called 'Daughters of the Sea,'" Efa said once they had gotten far enough out that they didn't need to worry about being overheard. It was a dark, foggy night, perfect for sneaking around in.

Jesse, who was helping Louise row, smiled. He was tall and dark-skinned and had a very nice smile. "I joined after they'd already given it a name," he said.

"And they couldn't change it?"

"'Children of the Sea' sounds terrible," Clara said, balancing their lantern on her lap.

"And I'm willing to be a daughter for a good cause," Jesse joked.

"You have no idea how much trouble it was after he joined," Nellie said.

"Hmm?"

Clara nodded along. "We'd had this nice sewing circle going for almost a year, and all our families thought it was great that we finally had some nice young ladies for friends."

"My family didn't," Louise said.

"Your family gave up on you when you started climbing on the fishing boats and going out with the men," said Nellie. "They said to themselves, 'Oh, well, that's it for Louise.'"

This seemed a little harsh to Efa, but Louise grinned along like it was an old joke. Then Nellie's words hit her. "Wait, you fish?" That was perfectly normal for selkie women, who mostly caught their own food, but human women didn't usually work outside the home unless it was absolutely necessary. Even Mary was an aberration in that way.

"What are they gonna do, try and stop me?" Louise said. "I'm good at it. A woman's got to make a living somehow."

"Anyway," Nellie said with a pointed look, "no one wanted us spending time with a strange man, especially when none of us are married and there wasn't anyone to chaperone."

"Is it required that you hold off marriage?" Efa asked. All of them except Clara were getting old to still be single, and even Clara was of an age, Efa guessed, to have a husband and baby. "To be a Daughter, I mean. That's very romantic, pledging yourself to a cause instead of a person."

They all looked uncomfortable. No one looked at her until finally Louise burst out laughing. "No, honey, it's not like that. They just leave when they get married. No girl's husband wants her sneaking off to secret meetings when she could be cooking him a good meal."

"It's hard," Nellie said. "Mostly they're still devoted to our cause, but they can't do anything about it."

"That's why we're such a small group right now," said Jesse. "We lost three last year, and now Clara's engaged." He shrugged.

"I'll find a way to come anyway," Clara insisted, but in a quiet voice that suggested she'd already had this argument and was used to losing.

"What about the rest of you?" said Efa.

"I'll marry when I please, and not a moment sooner," Louise said.

"She means," Clara said, "never. We're all taking bets on the sort of man who could sweep her off her feet."

"And I'm trying to hold it off as long as I can," Nellie said. "Dad's not a pushy man, and Mary's not my real mother, so I've got time. And we're thinking that once I have to, Jesse and I'll convince our folks we're in love."

Efa looked at him, startled, and Jesse gave a smile that was friendly but not particularly enthusiastic. "When I joined the Daughters, I went around to all of their houses and helped their mothers out until everyone decided I was a good sort. I can have my pick of the litter."

Nellie nibbled on her fingernail. "It's not perfect," she admitted, "but at least we could both keep doing what we care about."

Soon they were within sight of the island where Efa and the fishwives were staying. She directed them to shore and they all got settled on the rocks. Ninka and Afrit clambered on up into the lantern light soon after that, and the Daughters went absolutely silent. It took Efa a moment to realize they were all staring.

"Are these..." Nellie started. Her facial expression was obviously trying for polite interest but kept getting stuck on fight or flight.

"I must have forgotten to warn you. They're a little, um." Efa shrugged, like that could encompass teeth and tails.

"I'm sorry," Ninka said in the tongue she'd been using with Efa, in a tone that suggested she wasn't, "I don't understand you."

"They don't speak our language," Efa said, switching over so they could understand. Clara, who was probably the most sheltered of the bunch, looked a little bit lost. Jesse stepped across the circle and knelt to whisper in her ear. "Ninka, Afrit, these are the Daughters of the Sea. Daughters, meet Ninka and Afrit."

Each of the Daughters went around and introduced him- or herself, even Clara, whose pronunciation was shaky and involved a lot of looking at the others for confirmation.

Then Ninka stretched toward the sky, her body lit by the lantern, and all the humans leaned away. "Afrit is what you might think of as a siren princess," she said, casually, "and I am her bodyguard."

Afrit and Efa had to try not to laugh, but Ninka gave them a look that said not to ruin this for her. She just sat there waiting for a response from the humans, and Efa felt a little bit badly for them. They'd probably never even seen a naked woman besides their mothers and sisters, much less two, and in mixed company. The fishwives who appeared on ships or in wood-carvings tended to at least cover their breasts, and to look more like beautiful women than fish.

"Oh," Nellie said. She seemed not less shocked than the others, but less willing to let it overcome her. "Efa didn't tell us we were in such esteemed company."

"She didn't say much about you, either," Afrit said. "Only that you would help us."

"We're a secret organization that fights for selkies. To be a Daughter, you have to have a selkie parent. Most of the time it's your mother," Nellie explained.

"What she's getting at," Louise said, "is that most of our mothers were forced into it when they had their sealskins stolen."

Efa said, "Wait. George didn't-"

"No. My parents loved each other," Nellie said.

Efa sighed. She hadn't wanted to consider the possibility, not when George was their friend, not when he'd offered to help.

"She's lucky," Louise said. "Most of the time it doesn't go like that."

They stared at each other uncomfortably. Afrit said, "So, um, what do you actually do?"

"We support local selkies," Nellie said. "We try to make sure they're taken care of, and that nobody's being forced into anything."

"We're trying to change the culture," said Clara, and Jesse translated for her. "We want to make it so that it's as unthinkable to steal someone's sealskin as it would be to kill them."

"You must be breaking people out all the time, then," Ninka said.

"Ah," Nellie said.

"It's more complicated than that," said Louise. Her voice had gone soft, like she was breaking a hard truth to a child.

Ninka frowned. "Why? Your people have knives, don't you?"

Efa laughed nervously. "Ninka, we don't usually threaten people with being stabbed to death." But she knew by now that that would just be followed up with a why not, so she added, "Besides, you'd have to find their sealskins for it to work."

"And it's hard to convince people they should leave when they've been married to someone for ten years," Louise said. "Even if they're miserable."

Ninka didn't look like she believed that, but she was still so young when it came to people. Efa understood.

"We're never going to get her back, are we?" she said.

Nellie smiled an apology. "We'll try," she said. "If it takes years."

Efa nodded. The Daughters of the Sea were human, but now that she knew what to look for, it was easy to see the selkie in them. All four of them had darker skin and eyes than most of the humans in town, even Nellie, who was much paler than Efa. And there was something about the way the four had held themselves in the boat. Humans who lived by the sea needed it, but they didn't lean into the waves the way selkies did. Efa liked these people. She could understand them. She said, "Where do we start?"

{ 5 }

A STORM ROLLED INTO TOWN, CHURNING THE SEA. Louise sent for Efa to come visit her. Her home was a small apartment over a seamstress's shop. Efa had to go up a narrow, creaky staircase to get into it, and there were only two rooms, but it was clean and marginally warmer than being out in the streets.

"You can sit anywhere," Louise said, letting her in the door. "I hope you like it."

Efa squinted into the darkness that seemed to serve as Louise's living, cooking, dining, and entertaining quarters. The sole window was shuttered tight against the rain, and Louise had left most of her lamps unlit. The fish oil they burned was expensive in winter, when there was so much need for it. Efa got the sense that a single woman, with no family or husband to care for her, would need to save every scrap she could. "It's a beautiful place," she said. Bettan had always liked to visit with people in town. They'd spent enough time making small talk with mothers and sisters that Efa had learned the niceties of human conversation.

Louise apparently had not. She made a noise just barely too delicate to be called a snort. "It's all mine, which is what matters."

She slipped into a chair around the table. Louise sat across from her. "Are we going to stay here?" she asked. Louise had said that they were going to be asking people questions. Fishermen, people with connections, people who might know something about where Bettan had gone.

"Oh, no," Louise said, and then she smiled. Her appearance was stark, not a bit of ornamentation on her. Efa was a plain girl and not bothered about it, but still she liked bits of lace on her dresses, ribbons in her hair. Louise was as free of frills as a boy. "We're going to the Tempest."

Efa's mouth fell open, and she had to very carefully pick herself back up. If the Hungry Hogfish was the most reputable establishment in town, a place young girls could visit and remain unsullied, the Tempest was - well, not the least, but close. Fishermen went there and then spilled out the door, carrying mugs of swill and leering at anyone who walked past. They rarely did more than that, but Efa and Bettan gave them a wide berth anyway. She knew there were women who went there, but they weren't the sort of women that she knew.

"Really," she said.

"Don't look at me like that," Louise said. "I go there all the time and I've never had a problem."

"You do?" But of course she did. It was easy to picture her with the men, four beers into the night and laughing heartily.

"And you will, too. Soon you'll be an expert." She bit at her fingernail, contemplative. "Not in those clothes, though."

Efa looked down at herself. A nice dress, modest, a little old but well-washed and mended. "What's wrong with them?" she said.

"Nobody's going to take you seriously. You don't even have your hair up." Efa liked to leave it loose, but the town girls started keeping theirs elaborately tied up when they hit twelve or thirteen. No one had ever seen it as a problem before. It was just one of the ways selkies were different. Men were always complimenting Bettan on the wave of her hair, trying to touch it. "They'll think you're looking for trouble."

"I don't look like some sort of a-"

"No, you don't. But you look like some sort of selkie temptress, and we don't need the distraction right now." She crossed her arms. "You know you don't have to do this, right? I can take care of it all and then tell you what happened."

"No, it's okay." She wasn't going to let someone else do the work of saving her best friend.

"It's not like-" She took a deep breath. "Look, I'm not the eloquent one, I'm just the one who gets things done. But I'm not going to half-ass this."

She swallowed. "Thank you," she said. "Everyone acts like it's a joke."

"Not to me."

Louise was so still and small. Efa wasn't sure what it took for a woman to leave her family and take up a man's work, but she couldn't dismiss it.

"You said the same thing happened to your mother?" she said.

Louise toed the floor and grimaced. "Yeah, that's part of it. She's a selkie bride."

Efa didn't want to think about what could happen if they failed, but she was too practical not to. "Is your father awful?"

"I don't know." She got up from the table, leaned against the back of her chair. "No, not really. Not more than anyone. But - I can't describe it, it killed her. I don't know if it was the marriage or all the kids or just being away from the sea. But she's hardly even there any more."

Efa wanted to be sympathetic. She knew the right thing to do was to focus on Louise's mother. She said, "I can't let that happen to Bettan."

"I know."

"Really. If it was me, she, she'd tear them apart with her teeth. I can't just let it go."

"I said, I know." She extinguished the lamp and walked to the door. "Come on, Clara will get you fixed up."

They huddled into their cloaks as best they could, but the rain still spat in their faces. The walk to Clara's house was long, and the streets were muddy. Neither of them felt much like talking.

Finally they arrived at a grand house in a neighborhood Efa had never visited before. She raised her eyebrows. She didn't have much of a sense of human wealth, but she had assumed that Nellie was the richest of the Daughters.

Louise caught her looking. "Her father's some sort of merchant," she explained. "And all his sons work for him. They get along pretty well."

"All his sons?" she said.

"There're four or five. Handsome, if you're looking." She stepped up to the door and knocked.

"No, thank you."

The door opened. A little blond boy, maybe four, stood in the entryway. Louise smiled and he looked less uncertain.

"Is Clara here?" she said.

He slammed the door on them. They stood there, rain dripping off the tops of their hoods.

"You think he's coming back?" Efa said.

Clara opened the door next. She was wearing a velvety green dress and a tense smile. "Come in, come in," she said, her voice high and brittle. "My brother's wife and her children are visiting."

"I'm so sorry," Louise said, laughing.

Clara let out a breath, her facial expression frozen. "It's fine. I'm just happy to see you guys."

She led them inside to a room bigger than Efa's house. It was kept warm by a blazing fire, and there was - Efa could hardly believe it - glass in the windows. The boy sat on the floor playing with a baby while two women stood by and watched.

Clara, Louise and Efa stepped into a corner and talked quietly.

"We're going to the Tempest to see what we can find out," Louise said, keeping an eye on the older women on the other side of the room.

"Do you think that's a good idea?" Clara said, and Efa could have kissed her for it. "You're so tough, but..."

"Efa's got more to her than you'd think," Louise said. "But I think she needs to dress up a little."

"Like a lady," Clara said, and it was obvious that she was warming to the idea. Her hands were relaxing, where before they had been tightly clasped.

The elder of the two women across the room noticed them then. "Clara!" she said. "What's wrong with you? You'll ruin our floors."

She crossed the room in a few swift steps, and Efa realized with a jolt that she was a selkie. She didn't look it - she was wearing a dress worth more than Efa could ever have afford-ed, and little soft slippers on her feet. Her hair had been curled and pinned prettily to her head, an endeavor which must have taken so much time that Efa could scarcely believe anyone would bother. But close up, it was easier. She had a sad smile, and her eyes were as dark as the deep.

"Mom?" Clara said.

"Help your friends hang up their cloaks by the fire, and then get something to wipe up this mess with. They're drip-ping everywhere." She shook her head, selkie grace and obvi-ous wealth not enough to keep her from looking like a harried mother. "Nellie, Louise, I'm sorry about my daughter, I don't know what's gotten into her."

"Um," Clara said. She was trying to help Efa and Louise out of their cloaks, but it was a struggle, because they were both determined to do it themselves. "Mom, this is my new friend, Efa."

She startled at the name and looked at Efa for the first time. Clara busied herself hanging up the cloaks. "It's good to meet you," she said, voice unsteady. "I'm Clara's mother, Ffion." It was a selkie name, but she said it like a human might have. It didn't fit in her mouth.

"I'm honored, ma'am," Efa said. She was polite to humans out of habit, but she had been raised to respect her own elders.

Clara's sister-in-law was helping Clara find a rag to wipe the floor. Efa didn't like the way Ffion was looking at her, like she wasn't supposed to be there. She didn't suppose Clara often brought selkies over. "You're a good girl," Ffion said, as if to reassure herself. "How did you meet my daughter?"

"Well-"

Louise stepped in. "She and Nellie know each other."

Clara came over and cleaned off the floor, even surreptitiously wiped the mud off of Efa's feet. (Efa was too embarrassed to say anything.) She replaced the rag on a counter and came back. "We were just about to go up to my room."

Ffion looked Efa over once again. "You know I'm just glad you have friends, darling," she said.

Clara kissed her on the cheek. Then she led Efa and Louise across the house and up a flight of stairs to her bedroom. She let them in, closed the door and flopped down onto her bed. "Ugh," she said. Louise sat at her feet and Efa stood awkwardly in the middle of the room. "I'm gonna get it once you all leave."

"Sorry," Efa said. "I don't think your mom liked me very much."

Clara pinched the bridge of her nose. "I don't see why not. She likes Louise, even, and hardly anybody likes Louise."

Louise laughed. "Come on," she said. "Let's get to work."

Clara had a beautiful desk with a mirror on it the size of a small lake. Efa sat down and Clara fussed over her while Louise stood back as far as she could.

"You have such beautiful hair," Clara said, brushing it out. Efa had insisted that she kept her hair brushed, really, but that hadn't been good enough. "Do you want me to lend you a dress? You're practically my size, just, uh, bigger." She waved a hand over her chest.

Efa blushed. "I think your mom would kill us," she said.

"She doesn't need to be that fancy," said Louise.

Clara hummed and ran her fingers through Efa's hair, checking for knots. Efa relaxed into the chair. This was the sort of thing that Bettan had never been patient enough for. "Mom's not that bad," Clara said. "She's just watching out for me. I think sometimes she doesn't realize that I don't have a sealskin for some creep to snatch off me when I'm not looking." She stopped and clapped her hand over her mouth. "I'm sorry, that was an awful thing to say."

It was. But Efa couldn't bring herself to be angry about it. "It's scarier when it's something that can happen to you," she said. "And then it does, and it gets worse."

Clara started brushing Efa's hair back from her face. "She swears it doesn't bother her that much anymore."

"You don't believe that, do you?" Louise asked.

"I don't know. She says we make up for it, and that she loves Dad."

Louise frowned. "I could never love someone who'd done something like that."

Clara sighed and pinned a lock of hair into place. "We don't all have your strength of conviction," she said quietly, like it pained her. She looked down at Efa. "What do you think? Could she be telling the truth?"

Efa imagined that if she lost the sea, nothing would ever make up for it. "I don't know," she said. "I'm sure she loves you a lot."

"They say that once you have kids, you'll do anything for them," Clara said, uncertain, hands full of hair.

Louise started pacing, her feet loud on the wood floor. "But some things you shouldn't have to live through."

"I know that. What do you want me to do, magically fix things for her?"

"I don't think it would hurt you to try," Louise said. Efa brought her head down closer to her shoulders and pretended she wasn't listening. "Nellie can't, but I did, and Jesse's doing his best. And you sit around saying things like, 'oh, I don't think she minds being a captive in her own home.'"

"Maybe I'm not ready to follow your example and end up all alone," Clara said.

"Oh, is that what this is about?"

Efa cleared her throat. "Um."

"Sorry," Clara said.

Louise didn't apologize.

She had to ask. Bettan would have asked. "Louise, what happened with your family?"

For a moment she didn't answer. Clara said, "I'm not sure that's-"

"No, it's okay. It's just not a very good story." Louise sat back down on the bed. "I asked my father to give back Mom's sealskin."

"Nonstop, for a year," Clara said.

"And then what?"

She laughed. "He said no, obviously, and I couldn't find it. Eventually I decided I was never going to beg anybody for anything ever again. And I left."

Of course she had. She'd become a fisherman. "How old were you?"

"Eh, sixteen. So it was time. It's not like I was on my own super-early or anything."

Clara went through the drawers on her desk and pulled out a ribbon, then went back to Efa's hair. "It was still pretty brave," she said.

"You'll be fine as long as you can take care of yourself in a brawl," Louise said just outside the Tempest. She laughed at Efa's face. "Oh, relax."

Efa felt beautiful, but not very much like herself. Clara had pinned and braided her hair around the crown of her head, little red ribbons entangled in the braids so that they peeked out occasionally. And she'd lent her a pair of knee-high boots made of leather so soft that Efa could have used it for a baby's blanket.

"That's not very funny," she said, but Louise didn't seem to care. She opened the door and they stepped inside.

Efa could only understand the Tempest in relation to the Hungry Hogfish. It was darker inside, with fewer lamps, and smaller. The tables were crowded close together, packed with men who had chosen not to go to sea on such a stormy day. For a moment, Efa was overwhelmed. It was so loud. The air tasted like spilt beer and roasting beef. That was a surprise. So close to the sea, and with so many fishermen looking to sell their catch, fish was much cheaper than meat. The Hungry Hogfish only served meat once or twice a week. But she supposed that fishermen could bring home as much fish as they wanted, and were probably willing to spring for a little variety.

They took off their cloaks and hung them on hooks by the door. Louise put an arm around Efa's waist exactly as a man might have done for his sweetheart, with not a bit of caution or consideration, and led her up to the bar. She ordered them drinks while Efa took in the sights. No one had bothered to look up when they'd come in the door, and no one was watching them now. It occurred to her that there wasn't much Louise couldn't get away with. After everything that had happened with Ninka, Efa didn't think she could so much as hold another woman's hand without worrying about what people might think. And here was Louise, wearing pants and a doll of a woman on her arm, looking forward to spending a night hanging out with the men. It was almost beyond comprehension.

The barkeep handed over their beer. Louise took a swig of hers; Efa sipped. It was thick and bready, heftier than what George served at the Hogfish, but not bad. Louise slapped some coins on the bar and looked to Efa. "Ready?"

She nodded.

"William!" Louise called, sitting down at a table that was empty save for one man. Efa sat next to her. "Didn't expect to see you here. I'd have thought you'd take the opportunity to spend a day with your girl."

"She's my wife, now," he corrected, but he didn't seem too upset. William was a thready man, pale, with a face like a rat's. But he seemed friendly enough, and Efa could see the muscles of his arms bulging through his shirt. "And she decided she was going to take the day and make bread, so she told me to get out of the house before I got in the way any more."

Louise said, "Harsh. Did she at least keep you company for a little while before she decided to kick you out of your own home?"

He smiled and shook his head. "That's none of your business. Who's this?"

"Efa. She's my friend."

He peered at her from across the table. "Is she...?"

"A selkie? That's about the whole of it," she said. "But she's a lady, I don't want anyone getting handsy with her."

He held his hands up, palms open. "You know me, Hattie's my one and only."

"Then we'll do fine," Efa said. "Look, we're not here to hang out."

"Efa's friend was kidnapped," Louise explained.

He frowned. "Kidnapped, or–"

Louise closed her eyes like she had to steel herself. "Her sealskin was stolen."

"Okay, okay. I mean, I don't think that's good, either, I just wanted to clarify."

Efa clasped her hands under the table. "I'm just worried about her," she said. "It's been months since the last time I saw her, and she's my best friend. I want to make sure she's okay."

That seemed to steady him. "Understandable," he said. "What can I do?"

Louise leaned forward on the table. "We're looking for information. Anything you might have heard about someone marrying a selkie, anyone who maybe left town a while back." She held her cup with both hands. "Anything suspicious."

"Nothing?" Ninka said. "After all you did?"

Efa shook her head. "Not a word. Somebody knows something, but they don't feel like telling me. Louise is going to try asking on her own, see if maybe it's a selkie problem."

They were huddled in the lee of a boulder together, ostensibly to keep warm. Afrit had more or less adjusted to the weather, and had accepted a thick woolen sweater as a gift from Louise. Ninka said she would die, probably of frostbite, probably very soon, before she would stoop to wearing clothes.

So Efa had found a big, heavy blanket and brought it over to their island. It covered both of them, and better, yet, it disguised how close they had gotten. Ninka had fallen into the habit of putting an arm around her. Efa wanted it but she also needed for no one to ever know. Ninka was completely unselfconscious. It was something Efa thought she could learn if she had a lifetime to watch her.

"Does that mean I get you back?"

"I'm here now," Efa said, and put her head down on Ninka's shoulder to prove it.

Ninka made a soft sound. Her noises were so different from a person's - she didn't hum so much as trill, and sometimes when she was especially delighted she gurgled. "You're always with this Louise," and when she said Louise her lips and nostrils curled.

"I happen to like her."

"Hmm." She spoke into Efa's hair. "More than me?"

"I'm not sure," Efa said, voice teasing. "I like her because she's going to help me save Bettan. I like you for other reasons."

Ninka waited, her breath warm.

She grinned. "It's not important why."

"You can still say."

Efa liked Ninka a lot. She was petty and cruel and beautiful and brave. When Efa looked at her she felt aware of her skin and aware of her heartbeat and aware of the pull she felt, always, more than anything else, toward the sea. Bettan had wanted a knave to carry her off (and oh, it hurt to remember that) and now Efa understood. She didn't approve of Ninka, but she wanted her.

Maybe she was so scared for Bettan that she couldn't be bothered with what she was supposed to do anymore.

"I like you because your tail's so rosy," she said.

Ninka lifted the end of her tail out from under the blanket. The scales were mostly silver, but there was a streak from the tip of her tail to her hip that blushed pink. "That's it?"

"Isn't that enough?"

She took a big deep breath, whole body rising up, and then settled back down sulkily. But her hand didn't leave its place on Efa's hip, so she couldn't have been that upset. "I've probably eaten seals before," she said, vicious.

Efa laughed, startled, and kissed her nose. "You eat everything."

Ninka made a wicked, toothy face.

It was good to be alone together. There was no way to know when Afrit would come back. Ninka sang bits of melodies and Efa ran her fingers over the cables knit into their blanket. "You know I'm going to help you save her, too," Ninka said eventually.

Efa looked up. There was no way to say that Ninka was already helping, that she felt capable around her in a way she didn't with anyone else except Bettan. "How are you going to do that?" she asked.

Ninka shrugged. "I'll kill him," she said, steady. Something inside Efa solidified, and she held onto it with both hands. They would find Bettan and then Ninka would kill the monster who had dared come near her. They would be safe again, and together. Ninka would kill him. It was so simple.

"Do you go around killing people often?" She wasn't sure if she was joking.

"I don't know. Are you the sort of girl who gets all close to murderers?"

Maybe. Apparently. "I sure didn't used to be," she said.

Ninka squeezed her arm. "What do you want to do when we rescue her?" she asked.

She shrugged. "I haven't even thought of it. Not when I don't know if I can."

"I know you will."

She sounded so sure. Efa wanted to believe it. "Then - whatever she wants, I guess. I don't know. I used to think I never wanted to leave here."

"You've grown up," Ninka said, approving.

"No, I don't think it's that. I just - I can't stand them right now. I can't stand to look in their eyes and talk to them." She was so angry. It was only barely surpassed by her grief and her fear, all only barely kept in check by the knowledge that she needed to stop feeling and just do until she found Bettan. She bit her lip wistfully. "She always wanted to travel more. If she still does, maybe we could go somewhere."

"I'd like that."

"You just want to get out of the cold."

"Maybe." Her tail twisted under the blanket. "I could take you to the rainforest."

"I thought you said they weren't that exciting," she said.

"Not when you can't leave the sea," she agreed. "But you have legs. You and Bettan can explore."

"And that would be okay?"

"As long as you come back and tell me what it was like."

Efa was very quiet for a moment. "What are we?" she said.

"I don't understand."

"Around here, people decide they want to get to know each other and they - they court. And if that goes well, they marry. Are we courting?" she said.

Ninka looked at her oddly, pursed her lips. "What would that mean?"

Efa felt lost again, the way she sometimes did when she remembered that despite everything, she and Ninka had almost nothing in common. Not where it mattered. "When people are courting they spend a lot of time together. Maybe they kiss." She thought of all the people she knew, of Bettan and all her just-for-fun men. "Usually they kiss. You're not supposed to do anything more than that, though."

"Ah." Her voice was light, warm. "That doesn't sound like much fun." She stroked Efa's side with her thumb, and it took a lot of concentration to stay still and silent and to keep from melting.

"It's how we keep from making mistakes," she said. "It's not about fun. What do you do?"

"Whatever we want."

That didn't make sense. "Don't you commit?"

"If we want to," she said. She made a soft popping noise between her lips. "Look, I want to be with you. If that means we have to court and never do anything but kiss, I'll try it."

Efa blinked. "I just don't want you to - I don't know, get me to do all sorts of things and then leave like it didn't matter."

Ninka's expression went soft. "Of course you matter," she said. And then, to cover it up, "You're the only one I know who can survive a winter."

"I don't know a whole lot about selkies, I'm sorry," the man was saying, "but maybe you could help me?"

"What?" Efa said.

He was a young man with big eyes and rosy cheeks. He was at least their age, but he looked barely old enough to be out of his mother's arms. "I need to figure out how I can get myself one of them," he said. "It's lonely being all on your own."

Efa blinked. Louise had an expression on her face that was somewhere between horror and disbelief. Efa said, calmly, "My best friend had her sealskin taken and now you're asking me to help you take someone else's?"

He frowned. "Is that a bad idea?"

Louise sighed. She had increasingly less patience for these conversations as time wore on, and Efa was starting to worry that she would lose it and throw a table. "Thanks for helping," she said, and threw back the rest of her drink.

"Wait, but-" the man said. They ignored him and walked away.

The Tempest was quieter now that the weather had gotten better. They went in the evenings when Louise got back from work, and tried to leave before everyone got drunk enough to be a nuisance. So far it hadn't gone well.

"That was just great," Efa said a few minutes later, when they'd gotten replacement drinks and found a table. "This is never going to work."

Louise frowned, and it took Efa a moment to realize why. Then another man sat down at the table with them. He was large and crusty, maybe in his late forties, with sea salt dried in his dark hair. He had a mug in his hand and crumbs of the Tempest's coarse, nutty bread in his beard. His smile was as much a leer as anything else, and he focused his attention right on Efa. "I heard you were asking about selkies," he said, "though I doubt there's anything you don't already know." He gave her a pointed look.

She frowned. The men here definitely treated her better when she put her hair up and made an effort to seem a little more human, but when they noticed what she was - and it was inevitable, with her coloring and the way she spoke - they acted like she'd been trying to deceive them. She couldn't tell if she was.

She leaned forward and looked down, softened herself. Next to her, Louise was still, the lines in her neck taut. Louise was good at a lot of things, but Efa knew better how to be patient and gentle and womanly. "I'm looking for my friend," she said. "She had her sealskin taken, I think. Have you heard anything?"

He shrugged. "I hear lots of things. Which one was she?"

"Which one?"

"Of the seal girls."

Louise had her shoulders set and was staring blankly into the space between them. The man hadn't even acknowledged her.

Efa said, softly, "Her name is Bettan. Do you know her?"

"Dark hair, dark skin? Likes to dance?"

That fit half the women in her village. He could be pretending. "Sounds like her," she admitted.

He smiled like they were friends sharing a joke, and she felt very small. Louise drank from her mug and licked the beer off her upper lip. "Everyone knows Bettan," he said. "She's got that way about her, doesn't she?"

She nodded.

"And that would make you Eva."

She had no idea how he recognized her. She and Bettan spent a lot of time hanging around town, sure, and there were a lot of people they knew, but she was sure she had never seen this man before. Gefest would have said this was inevitable, that she hadn't paid enough attention to what was around her. Stupid. "Efa," she said, though there wasn't much difference. People misspoke her name all the time.

He didn't even blink. It didn't matter to him if he got her wrong. "You're a pretty thing," he said. "I always thought you were the plain one, but tonight you're really something."

She picked at the sleeves of her dress self-consciously. "Thank you."

"I guess you just needed someone to comb out that rat's nest."

She wasn't sure what to say. Usually when someone started to get on her case, Louise stepped in, but she was silent, giving Efa a look she couldn't parse. Efa tried a smile. "Do you know where she is? I'm worried about her."

"It's probably for the best," he said. "You had to have known that someone was going to make a move eventually, the way she went around."

She hadn't. Maybe that was almost impossible, maybe she had to have been phenomenally naive not to have realized. She had seen the way that men looked at Bettan, she had known that it happened sometimes, but she'd never put the two ideas together. Even now she could hardly believe it. Bettan was so strong, and everyone liked her. "You sound like you approve."

He raised his eyebrows at her. So? "I had a selkie wife once." It had to have been once. He obviously didn't have anyone taking care of him now. "She wasn't very sturdy, but she made up for it other ways. I'm not saying I wouldn't have married your friend, if someone else hadn't thought of it first."

Efa swallowed. It wasn't that she was opposed to older men marrying girls her age - George had a good twenty years on Mary, after all. She knew that a girl's appeal peaked young, while a man grew more desirable with maturity. But Bettan had always hoped for a man only five or ten years older, handsome and successful and wicked bright, someone who loved her for her charm and bravery. (Efa loved her for her charm and bravery, and couldn't imagine why a man might prioritize her beauty.) She had always expected that she would be able to choose.

None of that mattered right now. "Please?" she said. "I'm not trying to ruin her marriage."

Louise stood. The table shook, and then she had her hand on Efa's wrist, tugging. Efa got to her feet, confused.

"We have to go," Louise said. She nodded once at the man. "Great to see you again."

They stopped once at the bar to return their mugs, and again by the door to get their cloaks. Then it was straight back to Louise's apartment, and she was silent the whole way. They got inside and Louise sighed, lit a few lamps.

"What was that for?" Efa said. "He could have known something."

"He didn't," she said, setting down the last lamp. She looked unhappy in the flickering light.

"You can't be sure."

"Trust me, I know him. He was just going to mess with you as long as you let him."

Efa sat down. She had suspected that much, but she couldn't afford to discount anything. "How do you know him?"

"It's not important. Just stay away from him if you can, he's not the sort of person you should get involved with," she said.

"You never mentioned him before."

"He usually leaves me alone," she said. She walked around the table a few more times and took a seat with an uncomfortable smile. "I wasn't expecting he'd decide he likes you."

"I'm very likable," Efa joked, but she felt cold. She had to chafe her arms to keep the goosebumps down. "This isn't working. No one knows anything."

"I think," said Louise, holding her head in her hands, "that the people who know things aren't likely to tell us, and the people who might feel sympathetic aren't going to know anything about a kidnapping. That, or it's possible that she was taken by someone who wasn't from around here."

"So she could be anywhere."

Louise said, "I don't think it's likely she's left the kingdom. Unless a sailor took her."

She'd always thought it would be nice to be a sailor's wife, but it was a tough life. Efa couldn't decide if that would be better than being trapped inland, away from the sea. She couldn't decide if it was even possible for her to rescue Bettan from something so vast, when she was just a little seal. "I'm not going to give up on her," she said. "Not if it takes my whole life."

Louise smiled. It didn't do anything to make her look less tired. "I believe you. I just don't know what to try next. It's only going to get harder to get people to talk. It's been a while, they probably don't remember."

She thought about it for a moment. It was quiet except for the sound of people talking outside and the wind battering the shutters.

Louise sighed. "We'll come up with something. We'll search every house in the world if we have to."

"Okay," Efa said. And, "Thank you." Then she stuck her hands into her hair and started to unpin it.

Half a dozen selkies stood washed up on the shore when she returned to the island where she and the sirens had been staying. Her brother was standing in the middle of them, hands out the way he did when he was scared and trying to keep a lid on it. Efa picked up her sealskin and ran over to them.

"I can't believe she would do this," said a woman, still cloaked in her sealskin, her whole body angled towards the water. "To think that our own daughter would bring in these beasts."

There were murmurs of agreement, but another woman, so old she had lost all her teeth and had to be fed oat mash and mussel chowder, scoffed. "Whatever she planned, we can fight them off," she said, and everyone quieted to listen to her. "There are many of us, and, what, two of them?"

Efa froze. Nobody ever came to this island, she'd thought. Where were Ninka and Afrit?

"You didn't see them," said a man Efa knew as one of her mother's friends. "They could tear you apart without even trying. They move like eels, but faster than anything you've seen. What was she doing?"

"I told you," Rees said, sounding a little desperate, "they're not here to hurt us. I've known the whole time."

"And they're friends?"

"I've even spoken to them. Right, Efa?"

Everyone turned to her. "What happened?" she said, her voice trembling like a child's. Rees frowned.

"I saw - they looked like fishwives, but that can't be right," said the man.

Efa forced herself to stand tall and smile. Rees relaxed. She watched him, and he her, as they lied together. "Oh, those are my friends. They're very nice, just a little shy - I introduced them to Rees, but they didn't want to meet any-one else."

"She met them while she was away, remember that?" he said carefully. "She brought them here so they could see the coast."

She nodded. "They don't mean any harm, Afrit and Ninka."

She could see Rees memorizing the names. He was good at things like that. He said, "I'm very sorry I never mentioned them."

"Me, too," Efa promised. "We just never thought something like this would happen."

"What are they eating?" the other selkies asked. And, "They know they can't destroy the town, right? We get along very well with the humans, we can't have them ruining it." And, "They won't come near our children, will they?"

It took a long time, but Rees stood with her answering questions, and eventually they'd convinced everyone that it would be a good idea, or at least not an awful thing, to have the fishwives around. One by one the other selkies left, and Efa and Rees sat on the rocks together.

"Thank you," Efa said. She put her head down on his shoulder and closed her eyes. He looked down at her, and for a moment she thought he was going to push her away, but then he sighed and slipped his arm around her. "I couldn't have done that without you. People listen to you."

He made a soft sound. "It's not just me, you know. You think I'm this incredible person, but they like you, too. Everyone knows you've got a good head, and a good heart."

"Are you sure?" she asked, and hated how ridiculous it sounded. "Sometimes I think people think I've gone crazy, with everything with Bettan."

He didn't disagree immediately. "Lately... I don't know what to think," he said, and he sounded so tired. He seemed tired all the time these days. "What were you thinking, not telling me you'd brought a bunch of fishwives home?"

"That if I did, you wouldn't take it well."

"I haven't started screaming yet, have I?" He said so like he had considered it and chosen not to only out of great personal strength.

"I bet you'll tell Mom and Dad as soon as you see them, though," she said.

He laughed, and she pulled away from the sound, sat up tall on her own. She couldn't fight with and lean on him at the same time. "You think I'll have to tell them?" He shook his head. "Efa, by the time I get back there, everyone will know."

That hadn't occurred to her yet. She frowned and twisted her hands in her lap. "Oh."

"In case it hasn't got through your head, I don't know what you were thinking this time," he said. "Fishwives."

"They like to be called sirens," she said quietly.

"They like," he said, "to destroy ships and sailors. They're good for nothing. They live in the depths because they can't appreciate a day with sunshine and decency. Has anyone ever even hinted at anything different?"

"They're not all like that," she said. "Well, maybe Ninka is, and while I was there their king was slain-" Rees's eyes went wide. In the kingdom where they lived, the monarchy was stable, and had been for generations. A king did not need to worry that he would lose his life to plot or poison, and even among the heirs the jostling for position was relatively minor. Still, selkies didn't believe in kings, on the grounds that they were more trouble than they were worth. "-But Afrit isn't at all. She's a princess, like from a story."

"Why?"

"What?"

"Why did you do this to us?"

She thought, At least he still thinks there's an us. "Because - the stories. I thought they could help me help Bettan."

He started to speak, hands wild, then froze, closed his eyes, took a breath. "You can't just do that," he said. "That's not the way to get things done."

"What would you suggest, then?"

"Be patient, for once. Plenty of us would have been willing to help you look a little if you'd done it right - I would have, for sure. Act like a leader instead of a child, and maybe people will listen to you."

She meant to ask him how well that had worked for him, or why he was putting himself - anything - above Bettan. (She was his friend, too.) But instead she said, "How come you're never on my side anymore?"

"It's not like that."

"When we were younger, you would have covered for me even if you didn't think I was doing the right thing." She was worn from listening for clues and not finding anything, she didn't have the patience to be a good sister. "Now it's not Mom and Dad I have to worry about, it's you."

"I do love you, you know," he said.

"I know."

"It's just that you make it awfully hard to be on your side."

She faltered. She was doing what she could for Bettan - what she needed to do, no more. But he was right that she wasn't making it easy for him. "So what are you going to do?" she asked, resigned. "Tell everyone I'm acting like a fifteen-year-old?"

He looked at her seriously, then softened and squeezed her arm. "No. I should, but I'm backing you on this. You know that."

{ 6 }

NINKA TURNED TO AFRIT, SCOWLING. "I wonder," she said, "what she thinks she means by that."

Afrit wasn't normally vicious - she wasn't, anyway, wild like Ninka - but there was something to her that was cold. She examined her claws, which were longer than Ninka's and curved like fish hooks. Efa and Ninka waited for her. She clicked her tongue against the roof of her mouth. "I'm sure she didn't mean it like that."

Efa shook her head. "I meant it exactly like I said. I need you to be normal around them."

"I am normal."

Ninka was long and lean and sharp, her whole body bare and muscled, her gums tinged blue from the cold. Efa laughed hysterically.

"Do your parents usually dislike your friends?" Afrit asked.

"That's not - they'll love you." But Efa wasn't sure of that, so she pressed on as quickly as possible. "You just need to be careful how you act. I don't want you kissing me in front of them, or touching me, or looking at me the way you do."

Ninka stared at her, mouth open, for a moment after she finished talking, like she wasn't sure Efa was done. Then she put on a tart little smile and said, "If this is how you always act around them, I don't think I'll want to."

"That's not the point," Efa said. But Ninka refused to discuss it any further.

Efa's parents couldn't meet them at their house, though she thought her father would have carried the sirens over in a wheelbarrow if there'd been any chance they might fit. They met by the shore; her parents wore their best clothes, and she both felt pleased and wanted to assure them that this wasn't anything as important as that.

Efa's father couldn't help staring at the sirens, but Efa's mother was never surprised or intimidated by anything unless she intended to be.

"Afrit is our princess," Ninka said dully. "I am merely her friend and protector."

"I met Ninka first," Efa said. She wanted her parents to like Ninka. "I was very scared, but you would have been so proud of me, you couldn't tell at all. Ninka's a great warrior."

Efa's father barely smiled. "It's hard to think of my daughter being friends with any sort of warrior, much less a great one."

"I'm sorry," Efa said. "I know you don't think I should be doing any of this."

Her mother scowled. "You know why we don't," she said. "It would be so much easier if you stayed here and let it be."

"That's what I told her," Ninka said. Efa glared.

"But we talked about it," Efa's father said, "and you're grown now. Your life is going to be dangerous."

"You could die in labor," her mother agreed, "but we'd never tell you not to do that. And - we raised you better than to keep from doing something important because it was dangerous."

Efa stepped forward and threw her arms around her mother. She would have done anything it took to protect Bettan, no matter what her parents thought. But. "Thank you," she whispered, and hugged her father, too.

He said, "We just wish you had told us before you left."

"And that you wouldn't let this come between you and Rees," her mother said. "All he wants is for you and Bettan to be safe."

"All he wants," Efa said, "is for everyone to do what he thinks is best."

Her mother took Efa's hand and squeezed it. "You both have to live with your choices," she said. "I'm just asking that you forgive each other for them."

"How do you know all these people?" Efa asked Jesse. They were going around town visiting all of the selkie women, of whom there were a lot more than Efa had realized. She wasn't sure that it would do much to help her search - in fact, Louise had described the entire process as "wrongheaded," "a waste of time," and "just typical of you, Jesse, I mean, really, this is a girl's life we're talking about," - but she told herself it would prepare her.

Nellie laughed. "Isn't it wild? He knows everyone."

"After my Dad died," he said, "it was just the two of us, and Mom started spending a lot more time with other selkie women."

Efa nodded. She knew a lot of people who had been married to humans and had returned to living with their own kind. But it had never occurred to her to seek out other selkies in town.

"When we - the Daughters - first found out about him," Nellie said, "he'd been going around helping these women keep house for ages. We weren't sure if a son would fit in, but he wasn't going to stop, so."

The next woman they visited was younger than Efa would have expected for how old her children were. She looked maybe a decade older than Efa was, not even old enough that Efa would have considered her a real grown-up, but her eldest daughter was coming into young womanhood. She already wore her hair up, and her child's dress didn't quite fit over her form anymore.

The woman squinted and then broke into a laugh when she saw Efa. "Oh!" she said. "I'm Nerys, and," she reached out her arm behind her, and her daughter walked up next to her, "this is my eldest, Alis."

"Hello," Efa said, and waved. Alis smiled shyly and waved back. "Alis, that's - not a common name. Is she...?"

Nerys shook her head, and Efa got the sense that she was used to questions. "No, she's my husband's. It's not what most people do, maybe, but he loves me very much." She hugged her daughter close to her. "My children are very proud of where they come from."

Nerys sent her children out to play; proud they may have been, but that didn't mean that they needed to be exposed to any selkie influence beyond their mother's. "I'm sorry about your friend," she said. "I hope you can see her again."

"Do you think she's all right?" Efa asked.

Nerys smiled, and for the first time she looked like a mother. "We're women. Of course she'll get through."

"Yes, but-"

"She doesn't have to talk about it if she doesn't want to," Jesse said.

Efa didn't feel she'd done anything wrong, but she could recognize a rebuke. "I'm sorry," she said.

"It's all right," said Nerys. "You're scared, is all."

"She's my best friend," Efa said.

Nerys nodded, but not in a way that suggested she agreed. "That might change," she said. "Now that she'll have been married off."

"Her husband won't want me to see her," Efa guessed.

"Maybe." Nerys patted her skirt absently and, to Efa's horror, a hound stalked out from the other room and sat at her feet. Most selkies couldn't stand dogs. She had to work to focus on the woman's words and not the beast beside her. "Or she won't want to. It's very - your life changes. If she's lucky, she'll be somewhere like here, where there are plenty of other selkie wives, and she won't be alone."

"So, most selkie women can still spend time with each other?" Nellie asked. She had been so quiet that they were all surprised to hear her speak. "Even if their husbands have their sealskins?"

"Oh, I'd say so," Nerys said. "I know women who have to hide it, but they still spend time with us. It's an awful cruel man who'd keep his wife so alone, especially if she's young. My husband wants me to be close to the other women. He knows a marriage can't be just two people on their own." She looked fond and wary at the same time. "Still, I suppose that type of thing can happen no matter who you are. Any woman can end up married to a bad sort."

Efa wasn't sure she believed it.

But Nellie was still distracted. "So, you're close?" she asked.

"Very. We give each other advice, teach the younger women how to run a home, help raise each other's children - why?"

"Nothing," Nellie said. "It's just, I never heard of my mother doing any of that."

Nerys nodded. "Some of us are quieter about it. Who's your mother?"

Nellie seemed uncomfortable. "Her name was Mary? She was married to my father, George - he owns the Hungry Hogfish, in town."

Nerys smiled broadly, and Efa thought, thank goodness for these Daughters. She hadn't been sure it was a good idea at first, but if they brought people together, then that was worth it. "Mary!" Nerys said. "Yes, I knew her. Not well. She passed away a little after I had my first baby, poor thing."

"What a tragedy," Efa murmured.

Jesse looked at her and frowned.

"Did she..." Nellie lost her courage, then gained it again. "Did she have any particular friends?"

"I'm sorry," Nerys said. She reached out to touch Nellie's arm, but Nellie pulled away, and she didn't push it. "She wasn't close to any of us. It was - oh, but I'd never speak ill of a girl's parents, or some poor, dead woman. She was very sweet, and she deserved better."

"So, she was mostly by herself," Nellie said.

"Nel," Jesse said, very softly. "This isn't going where you want it to."

"That's no reason to stop wondering," Nellie said. She turned back to Nerys, who had as little to hide as the sea. "What did she do, then? If she wasn't close with any of you?"

"I couldn't say," Nerys said. "It's - Efa, dear, you should know this - it can be very hard to be married to a man. Most of them are kind enough, and you grow to love him, and you're proud to be his wife. But it has to be so much love to match what you feel for the sea. You'll be standing on the shore waiting for his ship to come home, and you have to remember that you took vows, it has to be your husband you want. Sometimes I think only what you feel for your children comes close. And even then."

"I understand," Efa said. She wondered if Nellie could, born without even a sealskin to connect her to who her mother was.

"But your mother was different from one of us."

"My father says he never took her sealskin," Nellie said. "That she wanted to be with us."

Nerys rubbed her fingers into her dog's ears, and it pushed its head toward her hand. Efa shuddered. "It wasn't a situation that any of us could understand," Nerys said finally. "It's not my place to say anything about it, and it's not your place to ask."

They went back to Jesse's place after they were done talking, and Nellie was very quiet.

"You've got to say what it is eventually," Jesse told her once they were inside with the door closed. His mother wasn't anywhere to be seen, but he didn't seem bothered about it.

Nellie bit her lower lip. "It's just what she said about my parents."

"She didn't, really," Efa said. "She hardly mentioned your mother at all."

"She knew of her, though."

"Sit, let me get you something," Jesse said, ushering them both to the kitchen table. His house manners were almost as good as a girl's.

Efa sat. Jesse's table was large, and perhaps could have been grand, but it was a plain slab of wood, undecorated except for the large crack that ran from one edge to the middle. It was possible his mother would have been happier if she had left her house in town and returned to the selkie village. There she would have been as well off as anyone else, rather than a poor woman who did other people's - Efa wasn't sure exactly, maybe their washing - for money. But she had a human son, and there was a place for him here that there wouldn't have been among the selkies.

"It's always like that. Everyone knows about her except me," Nellie said. She collapsed onto the table, her head piling on top of her folded arms, and Efa was relieved when it didn't crumble under the weight.

"What was she like?" Efa asked. "All I know is her name was Mary, and she married your father, so she must have been all right."

Nellie picked her head up. "My father..." she said uncertainly, or bitterly, or maybe hesitantly, it was hard to say. Wherever she was going, she changed her mind. "Her name couldn't have been Mary. That's not a selkie name."

"So what was it?" Efa asked.

"I don't know. No one's ever said, and I can't ask Dad."

"I think," Jesse said, putting some water on to boil for tea - his mother couldn't have been gone long, for she'd left the embers of a fire going - "that he'd be more receptive than you expect."

"I can't," she said, and Efa got the impression that they'd talked this over a lot. She looked at Efa and leaned forward. "I don't even know what I'm supposed to think of him. I don't know what happened, I just know everyone disapproves for some reason."

Efa shrugged. "Your father's wonderful, though. He's always kept an eye out for us."

Nellie said, "Yeah. And he's a good father. He was always there, and he's fair, and even when he got married again, he made sure we knew we'd come first. But I'm not sure - does this even make any sense? I don't know if he's a good man."

Jesse sat down next to her and rested his hand between her shoulder blades. Bold, Efa thought, for him to touch her like that, but then they were close. "You worry so much," he said. "You're the only one of us who knows your parents got together on good terms, and that things were good for them while it lasted, and you still can't let this go."

She covered her mouth with her hand. Nellie was strong, a woman built on a sturdy foundation, and she had flashes of leadership, but she was still coming into it. When she thought about it too much, when she wasn't just barreling ahead, she tended to curl in on herself. "Everyone says my mother was beautiful," she started, "but they say that about all selkie women, so I don't know if it was true. Dad says she was smart, like me, but quieter. She didn't like people much. I don't know what she saw in Dad. She liked to read, and he bought her books, maybe that was it."

"They loved each other," Jesse said. "They were young and in love."

"She was awfully young."

"How old?" Efa asked. It wasn't completely unheard of for selkies to marry even at fifteen, but it wasn't generally something people were proud of, and Efa disapproved. Bettan had gotten into all sorts of messes with boys by then, but the older Efa got the more that seemed like children fooling around.

"Seventeen when they got married. He was almost nineteen. It just seems like she would have wanted to have waited. I can't help wondering if they knew they were having my brother, and - I know that's an awful thing to say about your parents." But it didn't stop her from saying it.

Efa remembered the rumors she'd heard, the cruel talk that arose when a man's wives all died. "What happened to her?" she asked.

"My Dad's second wife died in an accident," Nellie said. "But Mom got sick. I was seven or eight when it started. I don't remember much before then. I mean, she was a shy woman. She mostly stayed home with us, but you can always hear the Hogfish roaring from any room in that house. I know people say it's haunted, and that's what did it, or that Dad killed her."

"I don't believe that," Efa said quickly.

"Me, either," Nellie said. "I'm sure he loved her. But sometimes I just want to shake him and say, 'Dad, you took a seal and asked her to look after your inn and your house and your children for the rest of her life, you might as well have killed her yourself.'"

Jesse touched her on her shoulder and she turned to him. "What do you want in your tea?" he asked.

She thought about it. "A lot of honey," she said, "but don't take so much your mother'll be mad at you."

"I suppose we can't all go to find your friend," Nellie said, poking at the fire. They were all of them, the Daughters and the fishwives and Efa, sitting around trying to strategize. (It was still hard for Efa to conceptualize a 'we' that didn't include Bettan.) "We have to have a plan."

"Well, who has the best history?" Efa asked.

"Um," Clara said.

"Yes, that's important," Ninka said. She was enthusiastic about the rescue efforts mostly to the extent that they were a grand adventure. But Efa also thought - hoped - that she wanted to help because it was the right thing to do, and because Bettan deserved someone to care about her. "How many people have you each rescued? And what happened?"

Jesse bit at one of his fingernails, and it made a loud noise as a piece came off. "There was that woman who lived on the hill," he said. "We almost found her sealskin, I know we were so close-"

"But then she had her baby," Louise said, toneless. "And she told us to stop."

"Why?" Afrit said.

Nellie leaned forward, resting her elbows on her legs and putting all of her weight onto them. "I don't think she felt like she could go back home after that."

"And we tried to help this girl," Clara said. Efa felt sick thinking of how young someone would have to be for Clara to consider her a 'girl.' "She wanted us to get her out of there, but it wasn't safe."

"Don't look at her like that," Jesse said. "We did our best for her."

"We still check up on her," Louise added, but it sounded like a justification. "Do what we can."

"He was going to hurt her if we didn't stop," Nellie said.

"I bet you she appreciates that," Efa said. She didn't know how to say that if he had taken her sealskin, he had already hurt her. She didn't think there was a way to put it into words that the half-human hybrids would understand. "Have you gotten anyone out?"

Clara held her arms tight around herself, back straight and nervous, a position that emphasized the expanse of her ribs and the slight angles of her waist. "It's important how you think about it," she said, and something about her, the way she didn't quite have the language and the way that her clothes and her hair said she had been loved but her twisting hands said she doubted it, reminded Efa of when she had first met Afrit. "We haven't killed anyone, I know, it doesn't sound like much. But there have been girls we taught how to bake, or how to weave. Or we've brought them jars of stillsap and honey, and that's helping, too."

"And honey - what?" Efa said.

The humans didn't seem surprised by her confusion, and that more than anything made her feel animal. "Stillsap," Clara said. "From the trees. It prevents quickening."

"Louise has this idea," Nellie said, "that sometimes they just need to be safe, and that's all we can do. And it doesn't have to be so dramatic."

"That's wrong," Efa said. "That's not-" She was shaking so violently she felt it must be visible to everyone. She couldn't explain the sensation of depth, her certainty that there was so much more beneath her than she could see and her frustration that she had to try to explain this to people who had never broken themselves into parts, who wouldn't have been able to knit their skin together except with a needle and thread. "You don't get to just do what you can manage and then say oh, that's enough, I did the right thing. It doesn't fix it."

The humans looked shaken, Nellie epecially, like she had been doubting something for a very long time. Jesse looked like he wanted to argue but hadn't come up with a thesis yet.

Then Afrit said, "No, no. You're right that it's not enough, and you love your friend so much. But it's not true that it's always possible to do more, and you can't tell these people they should."

"We are talking," Efa said, on the verge of tears and determined that she wouldn't break down and lose by default, like she always did with her brother, and furious with her friends and with herself that she had to worry about that, "about people's lives. About people's right to say no, and you don't even believe-"

"You can't talk to her like that," Ninka said, and the words rattled Efa like a net rattles a fish. "You have to listen."

Afrit looked so sorry, her tail twisting, and when she took Efa's hands her grip was uncertain. "This is the first time you've ever had something like this happen to you, isn't it?"

"I don't know what you mean."

"The first time you've ever lost something."

Efa thought of Bettan's parents, of Rees, of the way she had to hold herself apart from Ninka because she wasn't sure what was there. "I guess it is."

"So it's easy for you to forget that you're not the only one who's faced this. And if they didn't come up with an answer, maybe it's not because they didn't try hard enough - maybe it's just harder than you've seen yet."

Efa thought of the creatures that some said were found in the depths, tentacles as thin as a finger but that stretched on for the length of dozens of ships. She scratched at the ground beneath her, grit getting under her nails. It was wet and packed hard, more earth than sand but so mixed that it couldn't really be said to be one or the other. "I don't know what that means for Bettan, though," she said. "And who will help me save her."

"That's easy," Jesse said, and he grinned like a knave. "Whenever someone needs to do something stupid, Louise and I go out."

Louise seemed to contemplate this, and then nodded stoically, like there was nothing to argue. "I say we find the bastard," she said, "bind him to his own table, and net him through the paunch until he throws up his liver."

She and Rees hadn't spoken in days when he caught her on the beach on the way into town. "Hey," he called. "Wait up!"

It wasn't exactly that she'd been avoiding him - although perhaps, after her mother had asked her to reconcile, she should have done so - but more that she wasn't sure what to say to him. She grimaced and finished putting on her dress while he ran over to her.

"Efa." He hugged her, then held her at arm's length when she didn't respond. "Are we fighting?"

"No," she said. "I don't want to be."

"Then we're not," he said, like it was that simple. "I talked to Mom and Dad, and they said-"

"That we should make up. That's sweet."

"That you thought I was disappointed in you," he corrected.

Efa closed her mouth. "I never told them that," she said.

He ignored her. He was her brother; aversions and misdirections didn't work on him. "I'm not."

She nodded, and smiled, and kissed his cheek perfunctorily. "It shouldn't matter," she said. "You're my brother, and I'm too old to care what my family thinks of me."

"But you do," he said, and though he could have made fun of her for it, he didn't. "Are you going into town?"

"Just thought I'd see what was there," she said.

"Let me walk you." They turned so that the waves were at their back and headed toward the forest. "I can't believe you'd think I - of course I'm proud of you," he said.

"And angry," she said.

He looked like he was going to argue, but he didn't. "I was angry," he said. "I couldn't understand why you would run off without me and, ugh, I don't know why you thought fishwives would be better support than your own brother."

"I'm sorry, but they were."

He glanced at her, then turned his attention back to his feet sifting through the sand. "You just, you always have to complicate things, and I don't understand why."

As they entered the forest, the trees dappled the sunlight, and it was suddenly cold. She hunched over herself and they walked in silence, Efa trying to find something to say that was true - and more than that, honest - but that could be forgiven in the morning. "That's not fair," she said, all little girl little sister indignation tempered with a grown woman's caution. "You've been so awful lately." (And she didn't mean it, but she did.) "You stopped going places with us, and sometimes you'd talk to me like, I don't know, like not even Mom and Dad would say those things."

When he spoke he sounded tired, and hurt, and she felt wretched for even bringing it up. He spent so much of his time looking inward these days, trying to chisel away at himself and become something meaningful, and she hated to do a single thing to make him feel like he wasn't enough when he was.

He asked, "Why didn't you tell me?"

"I didn't know what to say. Or what you'd say."

"That I'm sorry. And I never meant to hurt you." He sighed. "You have to understand, I'm trying to be a good person. And I want you to be one, too."

"Well, sometimes," she said, "I just want my brother."

"I'll be better," he said, and she took it as he meant it. "Now, tell me about these fishwives of yours."

"What?"

He grinned easily, and she wasn't sure why she thought that it wasn't genuine. "You haven't gotten a chance to tell me about them, with everything," he said.

"Is that why you found me?" she asked.

"I'm just being your brother. You seem like you got close awful quick." And then, mild as the soft expensive cheese he liked to mix into his porridge, "Especially that one."

She was too smart to try to sneak. Rees was many things - sometimes kind, but always uncompromising - and he would cotton on to her. "Ninka?" She thought about it. "She's hard to be close to, but yeah, I really like her."

"That's good," he said. "Bettan would probably be jealous, but it's good for you to have other friends."

"She's nothing like Bettan," Efa said. But that felt both unfair to Bettan and too revealing of Ninka. "If I never see Bettan again the whole rest of my life, she'll still be my best friend."

"I know," he said, and she thought that he didn't quite approve. "I think Ninka means something very different to you."

"I admire her," she said.

He nodded. "She knows that this isn't your life, right? Right now, all this adventure is fine. You're going to find Bettan, you need to do that for you. But once you've found her again - Efa, she's already some man's wife. You'll want to find a husband, too."

"You're not married yet." It was starting to sound like an excuse.

"I will be, soon," he said. She tried to remember the last time she had seen Rees relaxed around a girl. It had been Bettan. But maybe he had someone she didn't know about. (She had, maybe, she hoped, Ninka.) "Oh, not like that. But you can't be happy without a real home, not like a wedding can give you. This girl's fine, I'm happy if you're happy, she's good for a friend. But I don't want her to keep you from doing what's right. Their values aren't like ours."

Efa made herself laugh, she shoved Rees away from her. "I'm keeping an eye on my values," she promised him. But she wasn't sure.

Efa hadn't been expecting to see much in town, but she was especially not expecting to see Ninka. Stretched out on one of the docks. Wearing exactly as little clothing as she always did. Talking to a man.

"Rees," she said.

He stopped whatever he was saying and followed the line of her gaze. "Wow," he said.

"What?" She frowned. The man's face wasn't pointed at Ninka's.

"I see your friend keeps reputable company," he said.

"I'm sure she's-"

"I'm not judging," he said. "But look at him."

She did. Before she had been looking mostly at Ninka - it was hard, when she was around, to see anything else. The man who had apparently made her acquaintance was not especially tall, but he stood jauntily enough to take up space. Ninka, curled on top of her tail on the dock, came up only a little past his hips. He wasn't wearing nice clothing - it was neither well-matched nor appropriate for any social scenario Efa could imagine - but it was brightly-colored, and therefore had to have been expensive. He turned, laughing at something, and Efa saw that on his waist he had hung a knife, curved and long enough that it reached almost to his knee. "You can't always judge people by how they..."

Rees turned to her, facial expression completely neutral, and waited for her to finish her sentence.

"No, that's, I don't know what to say." She covered her mouth with her fist. "Is he looking at her body? Because it looks to me like he's looking at her."

"You mean, do I think he's noticed she's not wearing any clothes?" Rees said. "Because I'm not sure, but if I had to guess, I'd say he can tell."

"She's not a bad girl," Efa said. "Sirens all dress that way."

"That's fine when you're at home," he said, "but you can't go into town like that. You can't trust humans to keep their eyes off you. They can barely stop staring as it is."

"Yeah," she said, and looked down at herself. Her hair fell over her shoulders and chest, which most humans thought was a deliberate effort to entrance, but her dress covered her from collarbones to ankles, and her sleeves went to her wrists. She wasn't wearing gloves (a human might have) but she thought she was respectable. "We should go help her out. I don't like the way he's looking at her."

"I don't think she minds," Rees said dubiously.

"I do."

He touched her wrist lightly, and she turned to him. "Are you sure you don't want to talk about-"

"There's nothing to say," she said. And then smiled, and squeezed his hand, and squared her shoulders. "We're good friends, I just don't always like what she does. You should know what that's like. You're the same way with Bettan."

The closer they got to the man of Ninka's acquaintance, the more certain Efa was that she didn't like him. He had a rough laugh, and when they came up to him, he smelled of booze and something that might have been rot or vomit. But he wasn't a drunk, either. His eyes were clear, not red-rimmed, and the slant of his stance was deliberate. He didn't weave, and his beard was carefully maintained. They came up beside him, and Efa saw him examine them out of the corner of his eye, but he pretended not to notice them until Ninka did.

"Efa!" she said, and she sounded delighted. She bobbed, body unsteady out of the water. "This is my friend Leon. These are Efa and her brother Rees - they're selkies."

"Selkies indeed," Leon said, appraising. He held his hand out, palm-up, toward Efa, so that he could take hers. His arms were lighter than Efa's, though still weathered, and the tips of his fingers were red. "Ninka told me you were lovely, miss, but of course-"

Rees slapped Efa's hands away from his. "She's my sister," he said unapologetically. "Ninka, you're friends with men like this?"

"We've known each other since I was very young," Ninka agreed, completely ignoring the insult.

"I might have married her," Leon said, "but I was already wed to the sea, and Ninka-"

Ninka, Efa, and Rees all stared at him, waiting to see what he would say.

He chuckled. "She wasn't inclined."

"But you should be happy," Ninka said. "I told him about Bettan."

"Great," Efa said.

"I travel a lot," Leon said, his voice low and improper. "Professionally."

"I'd gathered," Rees said.

Leon winked at him. "And a few weeks ago, I saw a man and a woman together. Newlyweds. She was a selkie, just like you."

"That doesn't necessarily-" Rees said.

"They were fighting," Ninka said. "And he said they were going to live inland. Didn't you say?"

"Oh, no," Efa said. "You have to tell me everything."

"Is that her?" Jesse asked.

Efa peered through the trees at the woman who had come out of the cottage. The three of them were hiding a ways back because, although Louise would cheerfully have marched up to the door and introduced herself, Efa and Jesse had discretion.

"She's beautiful," Louise said.

She was, but she was beautiful with pale skin and curly hair, beautiful like a scholar or a philosopher or a princess would have been. She was not Bettan, who if she had been a drawing would have been messy, the ink from her eyes spilling into the lines of her lips into the slip of her hair. This woman's skirts were lace and froth, they fell to her toes; Bettan wore her dresses to her calves, and hitched them up so she could climb over rocks, so she could show a man her legs. Efa closed her eyes. She felt like someone had taken a knife to a soft part of her, and all she could do was be still and hope the cut would come out clean.

"Is it any wonder you think so?" said Jesse, mirth in his voice under the caution. "She could be Clara's sister."

"That's not Bettan," Efa said. Her throat closed, and she sat abruptly. The pine needles rustled under her and pricked her fingertips. The brush around her hid the little house from view. From this height, she could not see the impostor. She wasn't upset, but she blinked hard.

Jesse knelt beside her, took her hands in his and stroked her right across the knuckles. "Hush," he said. "We'll find her."

"I thought we had," she said.

Louise looked around and then took her place next to them. "Rescuing this girl," she said, "will be great practice. Come on, I think she's alone."

They waited until the woman went back inside before they snuck up to her house; eventually, at Jesse's insistence, they knocked at the door.

The woman opened it, and it was clear that at first, she didn't see anyone but Jesse - her mouth fell open and she drew her arms about herself. But then she seemed to see the women, too, and schooled her expression into something hospitable. "Are you lost?" she asked.

"No," Louise said.

"A little," Efa said.

"We'd hoped we could talk to you," Jesse said. "Is your husband home?"

She looked over her shoulder back into the house. Efa thought of Bettan like that, some human man so much a part of her life that she expected him to be hiding behind her, and wanted to run. The woman looked them over one last time. She examined Efa closely, and her lips pursed. "I'm expecting him back shortly."

They stood there patiently. She laced her fingers together and watched them.

"How wonderful," Jesse said.

The woman caved. "Why don't you come in?" she said. "We can wait for him."

They introduced themselves because they weren't monsters. The woman said her name was Florence, though Efa didn't believe any selkie mother would do that to her child.

"What's your husband like?" Louise asked, subtle as always.

Florence stood up abruptly. "What an odd question. Would you like some bread? It should be cool enough by now."

"Please," Efa said.

Jesse tried again. "We're from an organization that protects selkies," he said. His voice was soft and steady, and Efa imagined that even a woman who had experienced the worst of men would be comforted by it. "We want to help give you your freedom back."

Florence turned to Efa. "Did you put them up to this?"

"No," Efa said, although in every way possible she had. "I'm just trying to-"

"Did my mother send you?" she said, and then, with more hate than Efa had ever heard from another selkie, "you look like her." She laid a basket of rolls on the table, and a crock of soft butter whipped with cool green leaves. "You can tell her I won't come back, and what's more I don't want to."

"We don't know your mother," Jesse said. "We want what's best for you."

Florence rolled her eyes, in all that lace a little tempest. "I'm not saying anything or going anywhere until my husband comes home," she said. "That's what's best for me."

"Yes, ma'am," he said, and took a roll. It was studded with seeds, or nuts, as a dress might be studded with pearls, and when he tore it open Efa could smell its sweet, smoky flavor. "This is lovely. Is it peppermint or common balm in the cream?"

She looked down her body and flushed in the very particular way of a married woman who had no intent but that her husband might see her be admired. "Both. My new sister planted me a garden as a wedding gift."

"And you're a selkie?" Efa asked. She said it to be cruel, and knew it, but it didn't stop her. There wasn't anything right about a selkie woman fussing over a plot of land.

Florence had a smile as silken and fluid as a scallop's flesh, and when the door opened and a man came in she slipped away from the table and fluttered over to him. It was at least a sea change before they deigned to recognize anyone else in the room; Efa imagined that generations were born and died in the time it took Florence and her husband to grow weary of a single kiss.

It was grating, like the itching of her legs under her sealskin, like the pull of her heart to the waves a long walk away.

Florence made a quarter-turn back to them, her husband's hands spanning the space across her waist and her abdomen.

"I didn't want to get to know our guests too well until you were here to join us," she said, "but Miss Efa and I were having a lovely conversation about her troubles finding a husband."

Efa thought: I don't want a husband, and I'm already being courted, and it was enough to startle her into silence.

Jesse looked angry for her, like he was going to say something, but Louise leapt to her feet. "We're representatives of Daughters of the Sea," she said, and then, looking at Efa, "and the local selkie community."

Florence's husband frowned and said, "I don't understand."

Florence whispered something into his ear, and he laughed. She hissed, "It's not funny!"

He held her close against him, the mossy curls of her hair flattening against his chest. "You're worried about my wife? And whether she wants to be here?"

"That's right," Louise said.

He considered this. "It's good that someone does. Roisin, if I get to chopping a cabbage do you think we can feed these people?"

Florence considered it, and butted her head against her husband's chest in a way that suggested that she was very fond of him and that he definitely owed her. "I suppose it's for the best," she said, finally. "They've already eaten all my bread."

When they made camp that night Louise cut a deep circle into the earth and dug out a pit for the fire. The soil here was thick and peaty, not dry and sandy. She could cut it into blocks with her knife and expect the blocks to stay whole when she removed them.

"We already ate," Efa said. And it had been a good meal, too, made warm and with pride by a woman who was glad to be a wife. Even if there had been no fish.

Louise looked very seriously at Jesse for a moment, then dug her fire pit a little deeper. "Has she ever done anything because she wanted to?"

Efa blushed and spread her skirts around her legs. "Is there any way I can help?" she asked. "Gather wood?"

Jesse bent over laughing, then stopped when Louise elbowed him with a thud.

"Go for it," she said, and used her hands to demonstrate the size she wanted. "Nothing that'll be missed."

Efa came back with an armful of firewood a few minutes later. She laid it by Louise and then sat herself. "Do you think we did the right thing?"

"Unfortunately," Louise said.

"We are," Jesse reminded them, "an anti-kidnapping organization."

"She swore she was happy," Efa said.

"It can't be about happy," Louise said. She had gotten the tinder smoking, blew on it with a smooth ease like a boat rocking. "It has to be about what she wants. You have to let her make her own decisions."

"That's fine," Efa said, although it wasn't, really, although she didn't believe it and although she had lived by her own decisions now and there was nothing to recommend it, "but do you think there's any chance she made the right one?"

"Of course," Jesse said, so soothing and so sure, before Louise had a chance to scowl. "Her husband seemed like a good man."

"Just like you," Louise said, and though Efa assumed there was fondness in it she couldn't quite be sure, "to think that the important thing in this is whether a man is good."

"He loves her," he said. "And he let her choose for herself if she loved him back."

"What a hero," Louise said, and cracked a bough in half so she could build a house for the fire to live. "Efa, don't ever let them trick you. There's no way a human can be a good husband for a selkie."

"Even if he loves her?" Efa asked. "Even if she's beautiful and - a woman can civilize a man, I know that." She thought of Ninka and her wilderness, Bettan and her spirit, how very much a woman might have to put away before she could think of giving the rest to a man.

"Has anyone ever taken a selkie man to marry?" Jesse asked. "Are your men good husbands?"

Efa thought about it, about Rees and her father and how scared she would be, dark-deep but different, if they were gone. "I suppose so," she said finally, "though why anyone would want to be married to a man who couldn't stand up for himself I can't say."

Louise did scowl, then, and she did it like a man who'd finished the keg and was moving quickly to the harder stuff. "You can trick yourself into thinking you're happy, that's all. That's all she's doing, that's all anyone can do."

"That's not fair," Jesse said. "I think my mother really loved my father. She was devastated when he died."

"Nellie cries every time her dog kills a gull," Louise said, and Efa wondered if she could be friends with someone who compared her dad - her dead dad, at that - to vermin. "That doesn't mean they were in love."

Jesse smiled gently, though, because to know Louise was to be patient with her, and he knew her well. "You're being difficult because you want to believe Clara's going to regret her choice."

"That's terrible," Louise said. "A friend should be better to her than that."

"Probably," Jesse agreed. "But I'm sure she understands." He handed her a handful of small twigs, and with her lips drawn tight she built them into the fire. "She didn't stop loving you, she just wanted things she couldn't have without marrying him."

"I would have killed for her," Louise said. And Efa wondered at women's love for each other, that Louise felt the same way for the woman she wanted to (maybe) marry as Efa felt for Bettan. She wondered how she was supposed to tell what was what, and if Ninka loved her that much.

"She didn't want you to have to," Jesse said. "You have to forgive her for that."

"What," Efa said, feeling selfish and not able to care, "am I supposed to do if we find Bettan and she's happy? Or she doesn't want to leave?"

"Maybe he'll have a brother, and you can spend your nights raising their pups and embroidering each others' shoes," Louise said.

But she would have done it, and been glad, because Jesse only made a tired sound, an old sound that reminded her of her brother and of their long-dead grandmother, and murmured, "I think you'll find that there are things worse than her finding a happiness you don't like."

Efa heard singing from the shore as she returned to the island, and thought: that's odd. She was sure that sirens must have sung together when they were among their own kind, so keen were their voices and so strange their songs, but she wasn't sure why. She had only heard them sing when they were overcome, either by anger that their hungers weren't satisfied or joy that they might be.

The waves washed her over the rocks, violent as winter came on, and she lumbered on, her flippers scraping cobbles. Ninka was sitting, or perhaps lounging, across the beach. Efa had seen orcas stranded on the shore, though she hadn't been able to convince herself to do anything about it until they were dead, but even though the sirens were nearly as unsuited to land they were more comfortable on it. Ninka was propped up, barely, on the bulging roots of a tree, one arm behind her head and the other clapping a quick beat with her belly. She was the source of the singing, and Efa realized immediately why she hadn't recognized it. She'd never heard Ninka so agitated before, like she'd been netted.

It took another moment to figure out why: Rees was sitting a good distance away, proud as a pike, his sealskin on his lap the only thing covering his nakedness.

He cleared his throat, and the singing stopped a beat before Ninka's hand, still keeping time, snapped on her skin.

"It's not personal," he said. Efa was amazed they couldn't smell her, or hear her.

"She's your sister," Ninka said, "and my favorite thing I have."

Efa thought that was so kind of her, to admit it mattered to both of them. Except then she said, "So it's not your place to take her from me."

Efa swallowed and sunk down on the rocks, her whiskers brushing against the ground. Either she felt like it wasn't their choice what she did, she wasn't a pup to be batted about, or she felt like she'd never been so proud as she was to have them both want her. Both seemed possible. She thought of Florence and wondered if it was easier to be married, to be able to say, "I'm waiting until my husband is here," and have everyone know that you had made your choices.

"She told me you don't have a family," Rees said, and even though it was true Efa felt suddenly guilty for how awful it made Ninka sound.

Ninka rolled her eyes. "You don't care at all what she wants or what will make her happy."

"I care about what's best for her," he said, "which is more important."

"Sounds like a convenient way to pretend you're in the right just because you don't like me," Ninka said.

But Rees had lost his temper, however much of it he had left, and if Efa hadn't known so honestly that he was a good man she would have been frightened of him. "I wasn't done talking," he said. "I would do anything," (and he said it like a threat) "to see my sister loved and happy. If she took as a husband a man who offended my sensibilities-"

"Even a woman?"

"Then, yes, those sensibilities would have to step aside. But you don't know her except now, when she's caught up trying to find Bettan. What you don't understand – Miss Ninka, I'm sure you're a fascinating person, and a good friend to her. But the reason she's so exciting to you now, and so caught up in this quest of hers, is that nothing matters to her like being here. With us. And when you leave, she'll think that she did something wrong."

Efa waited until they were done, and until Ninka had slithered off, before she shed her sealskin and climbed over to where Rees still sat.

"I knew you were listening," he said, and he pulled her close like it might be enough to make things better.

She was so grateful. He was her brother: she couldn't lie to him, and she couldn't apologize, either. But- "I don't like it when you fight with her."

"I'm sorry," he said. He scratched her scalp, his fingernails long but polished smooth, and she leaned into his head like a child. "It's just that I'm scared for you-"

"Then yell at me."

"And I can't bring myself to."

She thought about it for a long time, burying her feet in the sand and pulling them out again with strands of marram grass stuck between her toes. "I need you to be my brother again," she said. "Not my father, not my protector. And let me make my own choices."

"I'm not sure I can."

"Why?" she asked.

"Because," he said, "I think I know where Bettan is."

"What?"

"I'm sorry," he said, but this time she moved away from him. "I asked a man I knew to look, and – I can hardly stand to tell you at all, you have to promise you'll be safe."

Efa was so angry she stood, and she was shaking, and she almost screamed. "I can't ever trust you," she said. "I can't – you liar."

"I can't let anything happen to you," he said.

She wanted to throw something at him, she felt her hands clench around her sealskin. "You aren't coming with me," she said. "You don't deserve it."

He got up and stepped toward her, and she was so certain that he was about to hold her, to calm her down, to remind her how crazy she was being, that she was ready to hit him.

Rees said, "You're right. But please promise me you'll bring Ninka. Let her protect you."

{ 7 }

BETTAN'S MARRIED HOME WAS A COTTAGE ON A CLIFF OVERLOOKING THE SEA. When Louise stopped rowing and said, "I think that's it," Efa looked up and her heart twisted. It was perfect. It was exactly what Bettan would have wanted, romantic and so near the shore that the waves bathed its feet.

"That can't be right," she said, wiping her brow with the back of her arm. "It's beautiful."

The fishwives peeked their heads up over the surface. "You stopped," Ninka said, dangling her long fingers over the edge of the boat.

"I think that's where Bettan is," Louise said, and pointed.

The fishwives squinted. They saw well in the dark, and underwater, but not distances in the middle of the day when the whole sea gleamed with sunlight.

"I see it," Afrit said. "That smudge up there."

Ninka scraped her teeth over her lip and said, "I can tell we'll be very useful."

"We'll think of something," Efa said. She was trying her hardest not to get excited. If she got her hopes up and Bettan wasn't there, she wasn't sure what she might do.

They rowed to a small dock at the foot of the cliff; a boat much like theirs was already tied up, and near the dock was a path up the cliff. The dock was old, the wood weathered, but still steady when they tied their boat to it and got out. Efa and Louise sat down, their feet dangling into the water. Afrit and Ninka splashed, tapped their fingers against the boat, dove underwater and came back with clams.

Eventually Louise said, "You should go see if she's there."

"You're not coming with me?"

She shook her head. "It'll be better if we don't look like we've got an army. It's got to be you."

She had known that already. Bettan was her best friend. Louise was only here on principle, and Ninka and Afrit had come for the party. She crawled back into the boat and found her sealskin, pulled it out of her bag. It spread over her lap like warm butter, and she brushed the backs of her knuckles against the damp silkiness of it. "You'll watch it for me, won't you?" she said.

"All three of us," Afrit promised.

"With everything we've got," Ninka said.

Louise gave her a hand out of the boat. "You just need to find out what's up there," she said. "Come back down when you know, and we'll make up a plan."

The path up the cliff could have been better described as a climb. It was steep and rocky, with a knotted rope stretching the whole way for support. She thought she might never get to the top. But once she did, the cottage was less than a minute's walk. The land on top of the cliff was flat and grassy, with soft, sandy dirt and not a tree to be found. Towards the cottage itself, the pale yellow grass gave way to blue wildflowers smaller than Efa's pinky nail. There was a light, salty breeze, and to her side the ocean stretched as far as she could see.

She wrapped her arms around herself and squeezed, hoping for good luck. Then she knocked on the door.

Bettan answered, and for a moment they stood staring at each other.

She looked good, was the first surprise. Different, but good. Her hair was pinned up so that the tresses spilled over each other like waves. She was wearing a well-made, deep red dress that skimmed over her bosom and waist, turned her neat figure sumptuous. Efa could only imagine what the sailors at the Hungry Hogfish would have thought of that dress. But there was more, because she didn't look like a girl anymore. There was something in the way she carried herself, the way she looked out onto the world, that made her seem mature and mysterious.

Efa thought that she'd been right, marriage had changed Bettan. (It had been inevitable.) She wondered, what if Bettan was happy here, like this? What would she do then?

Bettan said, in a voice so quiet it could hardly be hers, "Oh, you've come." She threw herself into Efa's arms.

"I'm here," she agreed, and held her. She looked over Bettan's shoulder into the house; it was free of other people, and furnished with a new table and chairs.

She realized that Bettan was trembling. She put one hand between Bettan's shoulder blades, the other on the small of her back, and waited.

And soon Bettan stepped back, wiping her eyes. Now she looked young again, like the transformation into a wife hadn't been complete. She rubbed absently at her dress, a soothing gesture, and her hand was aquiver.

"I'm sorry," she said. "Let me make you some tea. My husband says I've almost got the hang of it."

"So you are-" Efa said, and then stopped.

Bettan waited for her. That was new; normally she was so impatient.

"Married?" She said it uncomfortably, as one spits out a piece of bone she has found in her stew.

Bettan pursed her lips, and for a moment she looked as though she might cry. Then she smiled, though it was weak, and said, "Yes. A few days after I left."

Efa stepped inside and Bettan closed the door behind her. "What was it like?" she said. Bettan waved her to a table and she sat down. "I mean - I'm sorry, are you okay? We can go. You could be gone before he even realized it."

But Bettan was putting the kettle on the fire. "I can't, not without my sealskin."

"You're sure he's got it?" She had been hoping, she didn't know, that this was all some girlish whim.

"No," she said. "I've never seen it, and he hasn't said a word. But ever since I first saw him, I've done everything he asks."

"He definitely does, then," Efa said. "It was gone when I checked for it, that was the first place I looked."

"Maybe," Bettan said. She checked her hair with her hands, going over it from temples to the nape of her neck and making sure nothing had come undone. "But it could be just me, or him, and not the magic. He's a very easy person to listen to."

Bettan had never found anyone easy to listen to. "You have to tell me everything," Efa said. "How are you?"

Bettan came over to her and hugged her quickly, her hands in Efa's hair. "I can't tell you everything," she said. She was trying to make it a joke, but it didn't quite work. Efa tried to imagine a Bettan who couldn't tell her things. It had never come up before. "But I'm - I'm fine, it's not as bad as it sounds."

"Your house is beautiful," Efa said.

"Yes," she said. And then, quickly, to cover her mistake, "Thank you. It's, really, it's more than I ever could have hoped for, given everything. Everyone's been very nice to me. I stayed at his grandmother's for a night or two before the wedding, because-"

"Of course," Efa said. "You couldn't have stayed with him."

"Right. And she made up a dress for me, she helped put together my linens. I always thought it would be you-"

"Me, too."

"-But I can't complain. They act like I'm his wife. I guess I am." She certainly looked the part, living in his house with the floors scrubbed clean.

"They said it would be good for you to settle down," Efa said, uncertain.

"Yeah," Bettan said, and sat down at the table with a little sigh. "I didn't expect anyone to come for me."

Bettan's husband returned a few hours later. The first thing Efa noticed about him was how big he was. She was a small woman, as most selkies were, broad of hip and shoulder but short, and he seemed to take up the whole room. As soon as he came in her eyes fell to the floor. She stood breathless, thinking, so much for keeping hidden. And staring at his feet - they were shod in shiny, soft leather, and easily two hand-spans long.

"Who's this?" he said. His voice was stern but not unkind, as a father would speak to his girl when he knew she had misbehaved but was inclined to be good-natured about it.

"My friend Efa," Bettan said. "She came to see how I was."

"That's a long journey," he said, and extended a hand. "I'm Paul, Beth's husband."

Beth? But no time for that. She took it and looked up at him. "It's good to meet you." He was young, in his thirties, with a ruddy round face and a full beard. His features were plain, not sculpted, but he was attractive in the way men are when they are older and powerful. She had always envisioned

Bettan marrying a man with inquisitive eyes and callused hands, but she had to admit that in their fine clothes, they were well-matched.

"And you. You must be very close with Beth to have come all this way."

She smiled, eager to please. Bettan was watching them, not unhappy but uncertain. "We've been friends since I was a girl."

He nodded, but absently, like she wasn't really saying anything he needed to pay attention to. She was suddenly, irrationally angry - he must have known that Bettan had friends and a life, and he'd taken her anyway - but she smothered it. "You can see I've been taking good care of her," he said.

Bettan piped up, "She was just saying how beautiful everything is."

Paul looked down at the table and they all waited. "You can stay," he decided. Bettan started to thank him, but he continued. "Although we can't offer much hospitality."

"That's fine," Efa said. "I'm used to taking care of myself."

Now that matters had been settled, he took off his shoes and jacket, placed them by the door. "Well, don't let her take advantage of you, she can run this place just fine no matter what she says. You can stay in the barn. Beth, what've we got for dinner?"

"I haven't made anything yet," she said like she wasn't sure that was the right answer. "We have some eels still, or I could kill a chicken."

"Don't waste a chicken, we've only got so many," he said. "Eel is fine. You'll eat it, right?"

"Efa," she supplied.

He looked at her.

She blushed. "Good for me. I'll eat just about anything."

Paul sat at the table, his feet up on the chair next to him. "That'll serve you well, with her cooking."

Efa looked to Bettan, but she didn't seem to have heard.

The eels were kept in a small barrel at the side of the house. Bettan reached in with her bare hands and pulled them out dripping and squirming, then prepared them in the kitchen.

"You should sit," she said to Efa, looking over her shoulder at them. "I've got everything under control."

Paul patted the table welcomingly. "C'mon, I don't bite."

She pressed her lips into a smile much as she would have pulled at the hem of a dress to try to get the wrinkles out. "I don't know that yet," she said, and took a seat across from him.

He laughed uproariously, and she relaxed. She didn't know what it was, because he wasn't a frightening man, but she felt safer when he was happy. "I like you," he said. "Are you married?"

It wasn't much of a question, but one she got often. She didn't think of Ninka, who was anyway nothing like a husband, and said, "No, sir. I'm the younger one, I haven't met the right man yet." She said the words carefully, placing them a great distance from the obvious truth that neither had Bettan.

"I didn't think so. Anyone who'd let you just leave like that would be a more tolerant man than me."

"Just me and my family," she said. She hadn't expected that she would want so badly to impress him. "What about you? What do you do?"

"I'm a fisherman," he said.

She squinted, because he didn't look it. Fishermen, regardless of age, were weathered and muscled fellows. They lived with the sea and its great joys much as selkies did, and they lived with the security that at any moment they might be swept to their deaths. Louise was a fisherman, with her strong jaw and her certainty in a storm. Paul didn't look like he knew his way around a length of rope, much less a ship.

"That's not really true," Bettan said, her knife tapping loud against the counter. "Tell her for real."

He gave a little shrug. "I own a few boats."

"Three," Bettan said.

"But I'm working on purchasing a fourth."

Efa nodded. In her town, most of the fishing vessels were owned by the men who fished them - a group of brothers or friends would go in together and divide the cost of the boat and its upkeep - but she knew that in larger towns, things were different. There one man might manage all the details while other men fished for him. For the fishermen the profits were fewer, but so were the risks, divided as they were. For the man in charge, there was little to worry about so long as the fish kept coming.

Managing a group like that, Efa thought, was lucrative and respectable, but not work. Not like hauling up nets was work, or slopping stew into men's bowls, or sewing a tired dress so it was fresh and new.

"So you're in business?" she said.

"Exactly." He sat very still, shoulders back, arms crossed over his slow-rising chest. "I still go out on the boats sometimes, like I did when I was a boy. There's nothing like the wind and the waves. But after my father passed, someone needed to take over."

"He's very respected," Bettan said. By now she had gotten the eels into a pot and was frowning at the rack of tiny jars of spices she had by the window. "His father - I never got to meet him, but they say he was a good man, a kind man."

"I'm sorry," Efa said. "That must have been awful."

"It was a loss," he acknowledged, "but it's times like those you find out who you really are."

"Of course," she said. She wasn't sure what he meant at all.

"I realized I'd been making a mistake. That I needed to stop acting like a child and do what was right for my family." He ran a hand through his hair; it was rust-colored and long enough to tie in the back. "So I took up my father's work, I found myself a bride. Soon I'll have a son to match."

Efa's eyebrows rose.

"Not that soon," Bettan said quickly.

"Soon enough."

"Darling, you'll give her the wrong impression." Her voice was light and shaky, like a bird out of the nest. She made eye contact with Efa, then looked back down to the pot she was stirring. "There's no reason to believe I - it could be months, years. You can't know."

Relief and nausea hit her hard. This was not what she had ever wanted, but it was survivable. They could find Bettan's sealskin and act like nothing had ever happened. But a child, that would be something completely different. Efa knew people who had stolen their sealskins back, some of them mothers with children. A woman could leave the life she had built, could break her marriage vows and return home, but she couldn't leave her children and be whole again. A woman was bound to her babies (even little half-human babies, who were born without sealskins and could hardly be said to be of their mother's flesh at all) as irrevocably as she was bound to the sea.

And there was no recourse for a woman who wanted to keep both her children and her self. The humans were very clear on this: half-selkie children stayed with their human parent.

It was something she couldn't let happen to Bettan. She was sick with relief that she hadn't come too late.

"There's no rushing these things," she said, and the look Bettan shot her was gratitude and terror.

The eels came out clumpy and jellied and, Efa suspected, undercooked. It was clear that Bettan knew she was supposed to use spices, but wasn't sure how much or which ones. The broth had a lemony, peppery flavor, but only once Efa got used to how spicy it was.

For the first few minutes of the meal, they were all silent. Bettan's shoulders hunched closer and closer together, like a scolded child's. Efa alternated bites of eel and potato carefully, thankful for her strong constitution. And, honestly, that potatoes were so hard to ruin.

Eventually Bettan crumbled. "I'm so sorry," she said.

"It's fine," Paul said, his voice completely dead.

"Really. I'll make it up to you. I'll make scones in the morning."

"Please don't," he said.

"Or those braided loaves you liked last time, with the nuts? I can probably manage those."

He put his hands down flat on the table, not quickly, but hard enough that they thudded softly. Bettan went very still. "Don't bother," he said. "It's fine."

She woke the next morning to the barn doors opening and the light streaming in. It was still cold and gray, and she pushed herself deeper into the straw that made up her bed.

"It's just me," Bettan said, and the door closed behind her. "You don't need to get up."

Efa pushed herself up on her elbows and looked around. It wasn't much of a barn, but it didn't need to be, when Bettan and Paul weren't farmers. There was enough room for goats and some storage, a few stables that looked like they aspired to hold horses when they grew up. She got the impression that they had a barn mostly because Paul thought he ought to. A wealthy man, should he choose to live away from town, would have a barn - and horses, and land, and men to tend it all for him while he was away on important business. Paul wasn't a wealthy man, though he was wealthier than Efa had ever dreamed herself.

"Did you come just to see me?" she said.

"Don't be silly," Bettan said, but she walked over and sat next to her. "I have the animals to look after, and breakfast to make." She grabbed a piece of straw and fidgeted with it. "You wouldn't believe how much milk humans drink."

Efa ate food other than raw fish only when she had no other choice or was tempted into it by particularly adept cooking. "Really?"

"He likes it in his porridge. Makes it richer, you know. Water just isn't good enough. Nothing is, you'd think he's a prince." She went quiet, then soft again. "I've missed you."

Efa reached out and squeezed her arm. She wanted to touch her, to make sure she was real. "It must have been hard for you. I can't imagine. Being all alone, and-"

"But I wasn't alone," she said quickly, cutting her off, "and you do get used to it." The way she said it, neither of those things sounded good.

Efa knew it was wrong, but she said, "You've changed so much. I can't believe you're getting up early to make someone else's breakfast."

Neither said anything for a moment while Efa tried to decide if she could take it back. Then Bettan said, "Well, I did need to grow up eventually." She gathered her legs under her and stood. "I can't stay, the goats need to be milked. You can go back to sleep. He won't be up for an hour yet."

She dozed for a while longer while Bettan milked the goats and fed the chickens, because what more was there to say? She had always been the responsible one, but now she was still a child and her best friend was a wife.

Eventually Bettan left for the house. Efa waited with her eyes closed as long as she could stand it, then got up, braided her hair, and went to join her.

Bettan looked up when Efa came in the door. She was seated at the table with her ankles and her hands crossed. "Shh," she said, with the caution, but perhaps not the tenderness, of a woman watching over a sleeping baby.

Efa closed the door quietly and found a place at the table. "I'm sorry," she said. "I didn't mean-"

"You were right," Bettan said, and she gave one of those sweet smiles that always made men forget she might have any wish but to make them happy. "I shouldn't have gotten mad."

"It's not that you've changed," she said. "It's just - things have. You're doing what you can."

At first it looked like she was going to accept that, but then she shook her head very slowly. "I look down at myself and I don't recognize what I see. Efa, you have to listen to me. You have to believe me." They were desperate words, but she sounded sure of herself.

"I do. I will."

Bettan's lips were a small, thin line. She held herself with her elbows and knuckles out, like a shield.

This was all wrong. She needed to take Bettan's hands in her own and run, take them both far away. Somewhere where no one would ever look on them with lust in his heart again. (She glanced at the door to the bedroom.) But Paul had her for his wife, and the magic in that was strong. If he had her sealskin, he owned her as surely as if he owned her bones. Efa said, "I've always believed you, no matter what you told me."

Bettan stood and fussed over the pot of porridge hanging above the fire. Efa knew this meant she was thinking, and that she would speak when she pleased. She had seen it dozens of times. She'd just never expected it from Bettan.

"I thought-" Bettan said, and then she cut herself off and closed her eyes. "At first I didn't think anything, I just, I realized I'd been taken, and you don't, that takes a while. You think people can't do those kinds of things to you, but obviously they can."

"If I'd known, I would have been so much more careful."

"Don't," she said. "Don't. We couldn't have, and that's not what I'm trying to say, anyway."

"Then what?"

Bettan bent over, her arms resting on the table, so she could speak very quietly. "I thought, they can take me away, they can make me marry this man, but I won't let them take over my mind. I'll still be me, underneath it."

"See," Efa said, "I knew you would fight it. I knew you'd be okay."

But she said, "No, you don't understand," and Efa felt like she was caught in a storm. "You change, you can't help it. I can't just pretend to be his wife but really I'm still free. Because there's - the fire needs to be tended, and someone needs to scour the pots, and his grandmother kisses me every time she sees me and says I'm her favorite granddaughter, and sometimes I try more than anything not to be here, but I am."

Efa nodded like she knew, when of course she couldn't. "We've got to get you out of here. Where do you think he put your sealskin?"

"Do you think I haven't looked? I'm just trying to find a way to be okay with this, I'm not-"

"You don't have to," Efa said, raising her voice. "You'll be free."

"I appreciate your coming here, but soon you'll have to go home and I'll have to make it here." She sounded fine, but she was breathing unevenly.

"I'm not leaving you," Efa said.

"He's not going to just let you stay in the barn forever!"

"Then I'll-"

But they both froze, because they heard the floorboards creak in the other room. Bettan recovered first - well, she had to be able to recover first, she'd been living with him for months. She put her finger to her lips, pretty as a doll, and said conversationally, "Oh, it sounds like he's awake."

Then she looked at Efa until she said, "Yeah, definitely, that's the impression I got as well."

Bettan made a face, the kind of face she'd make when Efa flirted badly, but with tension under the exasperation. She went to the pot of porridge almost as a nervous habit, stirred and tasted it. She looked the picture of a young bride, but her shoulders rode up high on her neck, and she couldn't quite manage a smile. "I don't think he heard us," she whispered.

And in the other room, shelves opening, a man shuffling across the floor.

"Me, either," Efa said.

"It would be okay if he had. He's not usually - he can be very reasonable."

"Of course." She didn't bother to say that he hadn't been reasonable about taking her in the first place, and was likely to be just as understanding about her inevitable departure.

"Okay," Bettan said. "Good." And then, when the silence had stretched so long Efa thought it might break, she called to the other room. "Darling, is that you?"

"Yup," Paul said. "Just getting up."

"Well, sleepy," Bettan said, and to Efa's surprise she sounded playful, "if you can be bothered to come out here, I'll get you fed."

He came into the kitchen less than a minute later, although whether that was testament to Bettan's timing or her cooking it was hard to say. Bettan put down her wooden spoon in the pot of porridge (her domesticity was a work in progress) and gave him a kiss.

It lingered.

Efa examined her fingernails and wondered how Bettan could stand to kiss a man who had done that to her.

Eventually they separated, and Paul took the seat at the table that had a few minutes ago been Bettan's. "Morning," he said.

"Good morning," Efa said. Bettan was scurrying around. She took the porridge off the fire, then distributed it among the diners. Finally, when she'd done everything there was to be done including wiping down the counters, she took the seat next to Paul.

"I hope it's okay," she said. "I brought honey."

Paul left after breakfast because "some of us have to work so you can eat." (Efa wasn't sure what he thought Bettan did all day, home by herself.) They spent the morning cleaning up, churning butter, not talking about how they were going to escape. Every time Efa brought it up, Bettan changed the subject.

And then she looked up from where she was pulling scones out of the oven, and said, "Where did you put it? You know it's got to be safe, right?"

"What are you talking about?" Efa said.

"Your sealskin. It would be just like you to get so worried about mine that you leave yours sitting on a rock somewhere."

"No, no, it's-" She remembered, all of a sudden, that she had promised that she would come back as soon as she could. "Oh, no, they'll think something awful's happened to me."

Bettan paused. Then she finished taking the scones out of the oven and wrapped them in a bit of cloth. "They?" she said, in the perfectly neutral and polite tone of someone who has learned to be very careful.

"My friends," Efa said. "They came to help."

"Who? Rees?"

She shook her head. "No one you know."

"I didn't know you had friends I'd never met."

At first Efa was insulted - did she think she couldn't meet people on her own? But no, she was just confused and scared. "You were gone, so I..." She hadn't explained very well, or in fact at all, what she had been doing all that time. "I found other people."

"Other selkies?" Bettan said. "Like, someone older? That's what I would have done."

"Um, not exactly." She fidgeted with her dress, with her hair. "They're half-selkie, though. Mostly."

"You asked a bunch of humans to come rescue me," she said, somewhere between incredulity and anger. "Really?"

Efa frowned. There were many selkies who would talk like that, but not Bettan. "You've always liked humans," she said.

Bettan raised her eyebrows in a way that suggested that maybe things had changed. "It's not their place," she argued. "It would be like inviting a man to a birth."

"Their mothers were selkies," Efa said. "They know plenty about these situations, they practically grew up in them. They call themselves the Daughters of the Sea, and-"

"The Daughters of the Sea?" Bettan repeated. "Wouldn't that be us?"

"Maybe."

"Granddaughters of the Sea, maybe. Distant acquaintances, more like." She was talking to herself. "They're barely better than humans."

Efa threw up her hands. "Bettan, they've devoted their lives to helping people like you. The least you could do is be thankful."

"If I get out of this place," she said, and her voice broke on the words, "it will be because of us. Not some human club."

"Without Louise I never would have gotten here."

"Louise," she said. "She has a name now."

Efa ignored her. "You'll like her. She's very practical, and brave, like you." She thought of Louise's pants, and how she'd probably never painted her lips to make them redder. "Maybe not exactly like you, but she's a good sort."

"What about the other one?"

"What?" She didn't want to get into this. "Louise is the only Daughter who came with me."

"You said 'they.'"

Efa looked away, tried to come up with a way to explain something like 'sirens' so that she would be believed and not cause any panic. "Well, uh."

Bettan completely misinterpreted her uncertainty. "Is it a boy? Did you get a boyfriend while I was gone?"

"What? No!"

She looked so delighted that it was painful to disillusion her. "I can't believe you. I'd thought it would never happen." Then something seemed to strike her, and she sobered quickly. "You have to get him away from here. If my husband realizes there's a boy here - if he found out you brought a girl to come take me away, he'd be mad, but if a man came for me, he'd kill him."

Efa froze. She sounded so serious. "He couldn't."

"Maybe I'm wrong," Bettan said. "But he can do just about what he wants."

"We don't have to worry anyway," Efa said. "There's no boys, just Ninka and Afrit."

Bettan tested the names on her tongue. "Are they foreign?"

"You could say that." And then, quickly before she lost her nerve, "They're fishwives."

Bettan burst out laughing and took a long time to stop.

"No, I'm serious."

"Like, sing a man to your breast and then drag him under with the weight of your snatch fishwives? Half-fish girls?"

She shrugged, suddenly uncomfortable. "I don't think that's what these ones do. But, basically."

Bettan stroked her kitchen counter like it was a child she wanted to soothe. "I always wanted to see the world, but you wanted to stay home. And then I was gone, and you decided to go on a grand adventure without me."

"Are you mad?" Efa asked. "I did it for you."

"No," she said. "I just don't understand why."

"Because no one was going to do anything. I thought - you know, they destroy everything in their path, they'd know what to do."

"Of course you did. You didn't know what to do, so you went and found some fishwives."

"They like to be called sirens," Efa said, and then giggled. "Come and I'll introduce you. You'll love them."

"Okay," Bettan said, "but where are they?"

"Down there," Efa said, and pointed vaguely in the direction of the sea.

Bettan broke it to her gently. "I can't go there."

"Why not?"

She sat down. "He doesn't want me by the water. I can't go past that trail that leads down to the shore."

Efa could imagine, maybe, spending a long time without even dipping her feet in the sea. She could probably do it for a whole day before she went crazy. "What do you mean, can't? Have you even tried?"

"Of course I've tried," she said. She stopped herself, lowered her voice. "Why do you act like I've just been sitting here going along with everything he does?"

"What happens when you try? Does someone jump out of the sand and drag you back to the house?"

"It's more complicated than that. I just can't." She wrapped her arms around herself. She was wearing a velvety dress that made her waist look thin as a needle. "You said you would believe me."

"I do," Efa said, "but what you're saying doesn't make sense. There's nothing stopping you, nothing real."

"It is real, though. It's like - when you're underwater, eventually you have to go back up to the surface, right?"

Efa shook her head. "I can hold my breath for a really long time."

"Yes, but - you can only wait so long, and then you have to go up. It's not even a choice, you just have to."

It wasn't like that, though. Efa refused to believe that anything could keep a selkie from the sea if she wanted to be there. "How long has it been since you...?"

Bettan clearly didn't like this line of conversation any better. "Since he took me, I guess." At Efa's look of horror, she added, "It's not as bad as it sounds. At least I can see it. And when I walk into town, that's by the shore, too. I'm sure once I'm a little more settled, once there are children, they'll want to play in the waves, they'll need someone to teach them to swim. He'll let me then."

Efa couldn't help herself; she shuddered. "What, is he scared you'll swim away?"

"I don't think so." She took a moment to consider. "I think it's that a man wants his wife to be devoted to him, not pining away for the sea."

"I'm so sorry," Efa said.

"Don't be. You should go see your friends. You should bring them a bite to eat, poor things." She stood and brushed herself off, walked over to the kitchen counter to look over her pantry. "Really, don't worry about me. I miss it less every day."

Efa walked down to the docks with a basket full of the scones Bettan had just baked ("He won't even notice they're gone," she had assured her) and a little block of slightly runny butter. At first, as she started down the trail, she worried - there was no one at the bottom - but the next time she looked up, their little boat had returned and Louise was waiting for her.

"I brought scones!" she called as she stepped off the trail and onto the cold beach.

"We kept watch for you," Afrit said, popping up behind the boat. "Day and night."

Ninka pulled herself up to the dock and flipped her hair. "You're late," she said.

"Sorry," Efa said. She sat in the boat and unwrapped the scones. "But I'm here now."

"I assume you found her?" Louise said.

"And her husband."

Louise took a scone and broke it open. "Her kidnapper, you mean."

"It's kind of complicated."

Ninka and Afrit were hanging off the side of the boat and staring at the scones, looking for all the world like a pair of unruly scavengers. Ninka's nostrils flared. "Are they good for us?" she asked.

"Did he kidnap her or not?" Louise said.

"They smell good," Afrit said. "But sometimes scent can be deceiving."

"He did," Efa said, "but now they live in a house together and she calls him her husband and it's just not what I expected."

"You try it first," Ninka said, "and then if you don't get sick, I'll eat the rest."

"Okay." Afrit leapt up and, almost faster than Efa could see, snatched a scone. Then she sank back against the side of the boat and took a bite out of it.

"You can't eat it like that!" Efa said. "Give it back."

"Mmrph?" she said, but obeyed.

"You have to eat it with butter," she said, cracking it apart and spreading some on, "like a civilized..." She looked at the fishwives, sand in their hair and crumbs in Afrit's pointed teeth, and gave up. "Do you even like scones?"

"Yes," they said.

"It's like bread, it has nothing to do with fish."

Ninka said, "We have very cultured palates."

Efa looked at Louise, who shrugged. "Make the fish some scones, then," she said, and from the way Afrit glared at her, it was clear that this had become a joke between them.

They waited patiently, at least, while Efa buttered a scone for each of them and handed them over. "Bettan's sorry she can't be here," she said. "She isn't allowed near the water."

Ninka paused in devouring her scone. "At all?"

"She can look at it. I mean, she's right up there. But yeah." She considered it for a moment. "I think he has a lot of rules for her that she just hasn't told me about yet."

"They always do," Louise said. She was the eldest of the four of them - at least as far as Efa could tell, when Ninka and Afrit seemed ageless - and though it was only by a few years, she made it count. This was Efa's mission, but Louise was in charge. "Have you started looking for her sealskin yet?"

"Um," Efa said. "About that."

"Did you look in the roof?" she said the next morning, after Paul had left for town.

"For the rest of the potatoes?" Bettan said. Efa knew that she was playing dumb. A selkie, separated from her sealskin, could think of nothing else. Efa could hardly stop worrying about her own, and she knew it was safe in the hands of her friends. "No, I haven't. It seems more likely they're in the root cellar."

"Bettan," she said, and Bettan looked up. As far as Efa could tell, everyone - Paul, at least, who was everyone in Bettan's life - called her Beth now, and she was always startled to hear her real name.

She sighed. "Yes, I checked over every inch of the roof. That one's a classic."

"The barn loft? It's got all those hidden corners."

"And the stables, and his tool box, and the haystacks."

Efa frowned. "What about the chicken coop?"

"I'm in there all the time, so I don't think he'd bother, but no. I even looked under each of their nests."

"Well, it's got to be-"

"And under our bed, and in his underwear drawer, and on the undersides of the tables and chairs, and in the summer linens we've put away for storage. It's not here."

"He has to have hidden it somewhere," Efa said.

Bettan looked at her for a moment, unimpressed. "Yes, you're right. Assuming he didn't burn it-"

"Don't say that," Efa said. It was possible, of course, to burn a sealskin. Difficult, because even months from being worn they were always damp, and smoked rather than burned, but possible. It was the only sure way to keep a selkie from the sea, but not many people tried it, because without the sealskin, a selkie could only be controlled in the normal ways. So it was a nightmare that only came true for a few, men and women whose captors thought they would be tamed if they had nowhere left to go.

"If he didn't burn it, and I'm sure he didn't, it's got to be somewhere," she continued. "But not here. I've gone over every inch of this property. I have nothing else to do."

"Where else could it be?"

She shrugged. "Knowing my luck? In one of those ships he keeps, where I'll never see it. Or somewhere in town."

"Oh, no," Efa said. "It's probably in his office. We'll never be able to find it."

"That or his grandmother's house. I haven't looked there, either." She leaned against the counter. "I could take you."

"He wouldn't use his grandmother like that," said Efa.

Bettan looked tired. "Yes, he would. She's his grandmother, she loves him so much."

Bettan's grandmother was a tiny bird of a woman with long white hair and knobbly hands. She looked like her bones might crumble under the weight of her dress, but when she pulled Efa into a hug, her grip was strong. "Come in, come in," she said, and to Efa's surprise Bettan seemed happy to see her. "Beth, darling, I haven't met your friend."

"This is Efa," Bettan said. "I told you about her. Efa, this is my grandmother, Isabel."

"You can call me grandmother, everyone does," she said, and swept them into the house. It was as nice as Bettan's, though bigger and better-loved. The wooden furniture was smoothed down from years of use, and everything was covered with bits of folk lace. "Grandmother, then." The three sat down at the table and Efa took the edge of the tablecloth in her hands to examine the stitching. Lace - even the rough stuff that common women made to adorn their houses, a far cry from the finery ladies used over every surface - was fussier business, and more work, than most selkies ever bothered with. But she had a special affection for needlework.

Bettan coughed, and she looked up, embarrassed. But Isabel was smiling.

"Do you like it?" she said. "I made it when my husband passed. A woman needs something to keep her hands occupied, when she's waiting for the kettle to boil and things get to be too much."

"It's beautiful," Efa said. "I can't make anything like it."

"I like," Bettan said, "how you meet my grandmother and win her over right away, but it took me weeks."

"I like you plenty," Isabel said. "I'll teach you both."

"Really?" Efa said, and then contained her excitement. "I mean, it wouldn't be too much trouble?"

She shook her head. "Not enough girls bother to learn these days, and I think it's a shame. Every woman deserves nice things, and heaven knows she'll never get them if she doesn't make them herself."

"I'm not sure that's such a good idea," Bettan said. "I'm not good at that sort of thing."

"It's not hard-"

"Uh-huh."

"-just time-consuming. It takes a little bit of patience."

Bettan looked dubious. "I don't have the patience to scrub a potato."

Isabel sighed and turned to Efa. "Was she always this bad?"

"Worse," she said. "Back home, she'd get bored if you made her sit down for more than a moment or two."

"I always assumed..." Isabel said, and then stopped herself. "We don't have many selkies around here, you understand. Beth was the first one I met. At least the first one who was still, I don't know, all wet. But in the stories, you make such lovely wives."

"I am trying," Bettan said.

"You are," she said. "And I wouldn't trade you for any of my daughters-in-law, the conniving little - well, you know that. But you're so unprepared for this. You can't cook, you can't take care of the land-"

"I'm learning," she said.

"-and sometimes I wonder what my grandson was thinking."

Efa wasn't sure, either. But this was no help. "Excuse me," she said, standing. "I'm sorry, could you show me the way to the privy?"

Bettan burst out laughing. "You sound so - just sit back down, you don't need to go sneaking."

She hadn't planned to go sneaking. She had just planned to carefully examine every surface (and, preferably, the spaces behind every surface) during a leisurely stroll. She sat.

Bettan rested her hands, fingers entwined, on the table. "We're not just here to visit," she said.

Isabel leaned forward. "I was afraid of that."

"Are you sure you want to do this?" Efa whispered.

"Yes," Bettan said. She rolled her shoulders. "Maybe. I need to know. Did he give you my sealskin?"

"No," she said.

Efa said, "How can you even know she's telling the truth? She could just be saying that."

"Because she's my grandmother."

"No, she's Paul's grandmother." She could tell from the look on Isabel's face that this wasn't the time or place for this conversation, but there wasn't a better one available.

Bettan was frowning at her. "And I married him, which means she's mine, too. I thought you said you would trust me."

She did, with everything she had in her. Bettan was just making it difficult. "I'm sorry," she said, though to which of them she wasn't sure.

Isabel ignored her; her gaze was all for Bettan. "Are you so unhappy here?" she asked. "We've tried to make you welcome."

"It's not about that," she said. "It's that no matter how wanted I am here, I can never be who I am."

She reached across the table and took Bettan's hands. "Who you are will change," she said. "Family is what's most important."

Efa thought: you're making the wrong plea. Bettan's family has never lifted a finger for her, she knows better than to throw everything away for you. She's smarter than that.

Bettan took a slow, shuddering breath. "I know. And I swear, I've done my best. But I just, there's only so much you can ignore yourself."

Isabel dragged her chair closer to Bettan. "Oh, Beth. Maybe you shouldn't listen to me, I'm just a lonely old woman. It's only I can't help but think - my husband dies, my sons die, and their wives are all nasty shrewish girls who wouldn't let me see my own grandchildren if I begged them. And then somehow Paul finds you, and it's like I have a family again. All I want is for you two to be happy."

"And I'm saying, I can't be happy unless I can be my whole self."

Isabel looked her over silently. Bettan wasn't crying, not exactly, but her eyelashes were wet and clumped together. When Isabel spoke, it was almost desperately. "Can't you find a way?" she said. "I know it will be hard. I know what you feel for my grandson now is only a wife's devotion, not real love, but can't you let that be enough? Just for now? It was hard for me, too, but I ended up all right."

Efa cleared her throat. "You're human. I doubt it was exactly the same situation."

Isabel straightened, like she had forgotten there was anyone in the room but her granddaughter and now needed to remember propriety again. "No bride knows how to be a wife when she says her vows," she said. She had that way elderly women sometimes had of issuing a rebuke without hardening her voice. "It was my father's decision, and in some ways I was as unprepared as Beth." She seemed to consider it, pursed her lips. "Not all, of course. Child, it will be easier for you if you learn to accept this. I know it's not what you wanted."

"At all," Efa said.

Isabel ignored her. "But it could be as much as anyone could hope for. You could be beloved, if you give it just a year. You'll never find where he's hidden it."

Bettan looked up and wiped her eyes. "You know," she said. "He didn't give it to you, but you know where it is."

She looked pained. "You can learn the cooking and cleaning. You can learn to love him. Do you really need to leave?"

"Grandmother." Her voice was shaking, but she sounded as sure of herself as she'd been in the old days. "He never asked me. He didn't even say hello first. That can't be my whole life, it just can't."

She thought for a long time. Then she said, "You have to promise me you'll say goodbye first. You can't just leave forever."

"I can't promise that," Bettan says. "You know I'll have to go as soon as I'm free. Before he finds out."

"I know he has a temper," Isabel said, "but he's a good man. He would never mean to-"

Bettan nodded. "I know. Please tell me."

She put a hand on each of Bettan's arms and squeezed her eyes closed. "I'll regret losing you my whole life," she said. "He hid it down by the sea, where you could never return."

"You can see why I love her," Bettan said as they walked back to her house. "She helped me out so much, I never would have survived this without her."

"She's certainly very talented."

They had stayed for a few hours on Bettan's insistence - though Efa hardly argued - to learn the rudiments of lace-making. "You can teach yourselves the rest," Isabel had said, "or find someone to learn it from, but the beginnings you should learn from someone close to you."

Efa took to it immediately. She'd been raised by good, respectable parents who had put a needle in her hand the moment her fingers were big enough. Bettan's parents had never paid much attention to her as long as she was quiet or, failing that, out of the way, but Isabel was patient with her, and by the time she was done she had made a single perfect leaf. She'd left it at Isabel's as a goodbye.

"It's a lot to leave behind," Bettan said. She was still smiling - she hadn't stopped smiling since Isabel had explained where the sealskin was. She was beautiful, even in that lovely dress Paul had given her, even wearing soft little slippers, even with her hair pinned and tamed. The only thing keeping her from her sealskin was time - well, and the tiny matter of actually finding it - and Efa was sure that once it was hers she would be herself again, barefoot and covered in sand and with hair falling like waves.

She didn't agree that it would be hard to go. Bettan would be leaving, what, a woman she hardly knew and a life she didn't want? A small price. But she knew other people saw things differently, and she tried to understand. "You're not going to change your mind, are you?" she asked.

"No."

"I mean - when we find your sealskin, you're not going to decide that really you love him, and you're happy here, and you don't want to go back and be just Efa's friend when you could be someone important?" She looked down as she spoke, dug her toes into the sandy ground.

"You don't think I can be more important than just the wife of a man who owns some boats?" Bettan said, laughing.

"That's not what I-"

"Hush, hush." She took Efa's hand and squeezed it, then let go. "No, I'm sure. You have no idea how often - how many times it would have been easier if I'd loved him. Maybe if he'd asked, or if we'd known each other first."

"You wouldn't have," Efa said. "He's a brute."

Bettan gave her an odd look. "He hasn't done anything to you, has he?"

"No. Except he doesn't treat you right."

She nodded, seemed to take that for what it was.

It was still early afternoon when they got back to the house. Efa had expected Bettan would dampen again when they got to the house, but it seemed that the promise of getting her sealskin back had elevated her. Once Efa had caught an awful chest cold, and for weeks she could take no more than the slightest of breaths without coughing until she choked. She remembered after, being able to breathe again, and thought maybe that was how Bettan felt.

"I should probably get my things," Bettan said. Her smile suggested that she wasn't really there anymore, that in all the important ways she had already left.

"I can help," Efa said, but Bettan pushed her away.

"Go look," she said. "I'll be waiting."

"It's down here?" Louise said when she found out. She was furious. "It's been right here this whole time and it never occurred to me?"

They looked everywhere. In the little tool shack on the shore, which was full of things to keep the dock and boat in good standing, but had no sealskin. The fishwives examined every bit of the dock and found it completely ordinary. Efa was pacing the dock when a lock caught her eye.

Locks were expensive, and hardly anyone ever needed one.

"Louise," she said. She spoke softly, but her voice carried over the shore. "Do you think he would...?"

Ninka and Afrit perked up and came over to watch. Louise, who had been sitting on the edge of the dock with her legs hanging over the side, stood and followed Efa's gaze. "That bastard," she said.

They hadn't paid much attention to the boat Paul had tied to the dock. It was much like theirs, but a little nicer. Efa couldn't dream what he did with it, but she knew him well enough to know that he was a man who liked to have nice things he didn't use. There was a small wooden crate in the boat, but she had never paid attention to it before. There was one in their boat, too, to store supplies - food and water, a length of rope, a knife - in case they got lost or pulled out to sea. But theirs wasn't locked.

Louise scrambled over to Paul's boat and knelt next to the crate. She waved Efa over.

"I didn't think it would be locked," Efa said mournfully. "Hidden, obviously, but-"

"There's always a way," Louise said. "Give me a minute." Then she left for the shore, and disappeared into the tool shed.

Someone coughed. Efa turned and saw Afrit watching her. Ninka was further back - she had grown quiet in these past few days, when it had become apparent that rescuing Bettan was not going to be the adventure she had hoped for. "Is everything all right?" Afrit asked.

"Yeah," she said, and then corrected herself. "I think it's in this box, but it's locked."

Afrit's pupils widened, but she was wearing one of those opaque siren expressions, and Efa couldn't begin to guess at what she meant by it. "Ah," she said, which was about as helpful as the pupil thing. Loud banging and crashing noises came from the tool shack. "Well, as you know, you have us around just as soon as you need something involving riddles or catching fish or swimming or-"

"Thank you," Efa said. She turned back to examining the lock. As far as she could tell, it was well-made - he must have had it done specially for him. He must have had everything planned out before the first time he even saw Bettan. That was a hard realization, and sat uneasily in her stomach. None of this had anything to do with them, not in particular.

The sound of footsteps made her look up. Louise strutted down the length of the dock, a crowbar thrown over her shoulder. She looked pleased; she was always happiest to have something to do. "I knew I saw this baby in there," she said.

"I'm not sure the lock will break," Efa said. "It looks pretty secure."

Louise shrugged. "If I go at it hard enough, something's going to give. I don't really care if it's the lock or the crate. Now, get out of the way."

Efa and the fishwives moved a safe distance away to watch. Ninka took up a spot behind Efa, and she wrapped her long, clawed fingers around Efa's. "Are you happy?" she asked. "You're going to bring your friend home."

Louise jammed the tip of the crowbar into the crate and put all her weight on it, her muscles bulging like a man's.

"I don't know," Efa said. She took her hand, Ninka's laced around it, and pulled it across her belly, so that Ninka was holding her. She laughed. "I'm terrified."

Ninka made a noise, high and gurgling, the kind of noise a monster makes to its children. "That's normal. Humans and selkies are always a little scared."

"But not sirens?"

"Never," she said. "We were born for adventure."

Louise turned to the three of them. She hadn't yet started to work up a sweat, but that was more a testament to the cool weather than anything else. "It's a good thing you all have me to do your hard work for you," she said.

"We're supervising," Afrit informed her haughtily.

Louise grinned. "I think it's just about to... there," she said, and the wood creaked loudly. She shoved the crowbar deeper into the crate, and after a bit more jimmying she was able to bend forward and pull the top off.

Efa hurried to her feet and came over. "Is it-?" she said.

And there it was, dusty but still shimmering in the sun. She couldn't help herself - she bent and grabbed the sealskin, stroking it compulsively as it spilled out over her arms. "I have to go," she said. "She'll want to hold it as soon as she can." She smiled, feeling for the first time in days like things would be okay. They could swim back home beside the boat, and no one would ever separate them from their sealskins again.

"Bettan!" she called when she got to the house. "I've got it! Come on, we'll-"

And then she stopped, because she had opened the door. Inside, Paul sat at the table.

It took her a moment longer, in her horror, to locate Bettan. She was at the counter chopping vegetables. She looked up at Efa and mouthed "I'm sorry."

"Efa," Paul said. He sounded neither surprised nor pleased. "Where have you been off to? Beth wasn't able to give me a satisfactory answer."

She froze in the doorway, then cleared her throat. "Just out," she said. She moved Bettan's sealskin behind her as discreetly as she could.

Not discreetly enough. "What's that?" he said.

"Nothing."

He stood, and she was aware to her bones of how much bigger he was. Big hands, big feet. "Did you find the-" And she must have looked guilty, because he cut himself off. "Give it to me."

Her hands tightened on the sealskin, but she didn't say anything.

"Efa," he said, like he was talking to a disobedient child, "I'm about to get frustrated."

"Stop," Bettan said. She turned to face them both, the knife still in her hand. "She found my sealskin. That means I get to go free."

He laughed. "You're my wife," he said. "You belong with me."

Efa expected that to be the end of it. Bettan had become so easy to push aside. But she didn't budge. "I don't want to be your wife anymore, Paul," she said. Efa realized that it was the first time she had ever heard her use his name. And then she corrected herself: "I never wanted to be your wife."

He waited her out, eyebrows raised, unimpressed. No one said anything for a long while. Then he turned to Efa and said, very softly, "We need to have a private chat. Why don't you give me the skin and wander off somewhere?"

She shook her head. He sighed - such a slight thing, like a songbird - and walked over to her. She knew she would be ashamed of it the rest of her life, but she couldn't move. (She didn't believe that this was happening, that he knew what they wanted and didn't care.) She thought, he's going to stop any second now. And then, when it became obvious that he wasn't, she thought, Bettan is going to stop him.

He stood right in front of her and put his hand on her arm, cupping her elbow. He held out his other hand and waited for her to give it to him.

She thought of all the time she'd spent trying to learn how to fight. And then she ran.

She ran as fast as she could, out the door, barefoot through the sandy grass and wildflowers. Bettan followed her, and somehow managed to catch up in her slippers. The sea stretched out to their side, and Efa kept telling herself they just needed to get that far and they would be free. She looked over - Bettan was determined and terrified and finally, stutteringly free - and behind them. Paul was so close she wished she hadn't. They were stronger, and faster, but he had longer legs.

He caught up to them, and as she prepared to push him away she realized she'd guessed wrong. She'd thought he would take the sealskin above all else - take it and burn it, probably, or shred it into pieces and hang them on his wall. But when given the choice between reaching for the sealskin and for Bettan, he grabbed the one he really wanted.

Bettan shrieked and crashed, Paul on top of her, into the ground.

Efa whirled, the sealskin clutched to her chest, and she screamed, too. She held her breath and backed away, watching as Bettan wrestled out from under him and scrambled to her feet. He held on tight to her wrist, but that didn't last long because -

(Efa gasped and covered her face, but not her eyes.)

- she had never put down the knife.

She hacked at his arm like she was chopping firewood. He made a noise, more surprise than pain, and dropped her wrist. She was off before Efa even saw blood, and this time they had a lead.

They slipped down the path to the water. The rope burned Efa's hand as she held on, and her feet crashed into rocks, but she couldn't stop. "Do you think he's-"

"Yes," Bettan said. "Go."

Efa didn't look back until they made it to the beach. He was a ways back, stumbling down the switchbacks of the cliff path. She smiled. He was human, he wasn't as nimble as they were. Louise was untying her boat from the dock. Efa couldn't see the fishwives, but she knew they tended to lurk.

They sprinted down the dock to Louise. She already had Efa's sealskin ready, and handed it over. She nodded at Bettan. "You've got to hurry."

Bettan tossed the knife into the rowboat and took her sealskin back. They both stripped. Bettan's fine dress, down to her feet and with tiny laces, tore as she yanked it over her head. The dresses went in the boat, and they both started to unfold their sealskins.

"I've got to go," Louise said. She was the only one who couldn't just swim away, and though she was strong as a man, she probably couldn't row faster than one. And Paul was on the beach now, shouting as he ran. Efa thought she would have understood him if she hadn't been so scared.

"Thank you," Efa said. She and Bettan bent and pushed the boat off. Louise hurried away. Then, with a final look over her shoulder, Efa jumped into the sea.

All her fear left her as soon as she touched the water, felt Bettan splash beside her. There were men who could trap a seal in its natural habitat, but - she was sure of this - Paul was not one of those men. She had been maneuvering in the water all her life. She slipped her feet into her sealskin and pulled it up around her, eyes closed, bubbles coming out her nose. Soon she was herself again.

But Bettan wasn't.

She had pulled her sealskin around herself like a shield, and she wriggled around inside of it, but it didn't bond to her skin. Had she forgotten how? But that didn't make sense. It wasn't something a person could forget.

Paul slid into the water behind her.

She kicked and tried to swim away, but there wasn't much she could do with her legs trapped in the sealskin. He grabbed onto her by the shoulders, and she thrashed help-lessly. His feet could touch the ground at this depth; hers couldn't. Her sealskin fell from her body and she was naked. She screamed and sputtered (even through the water, Efa could hear her) but she couldn't breathe - he held her down, completely submerged. Her arms and shoulders were dimpled with the force he used to hold her, and her skin was mottled with bruises over the meat of her thighs and the curve of her ribs.

Efa swam towards her, not even sure what she was going to do.

And then from out of the depths came Ninka. Paul couldn't have predicted her, she was just there. She plucked him up exactly as Efa would have grabbed a small bug: firmly, with the sharp tips of her fingers piercing his sides. Efa had once asked Ninka if she'd ever killed a man, and Ninka hadn't offered a clear answer. But it was clear she meant to, now. Paul writhed in her claws, twisting in a futile attempt to see who - what - had gotten him, but she only dug in deeper. He had been able to overpower Bettan and intimidate her, but Ninka had never needed to be afraid.

He let Bettan go. She dove for her sealskin and then swam away as fast as she could.

Efa couldn't let him ever get near her again. Because finally she knew what, perhaps, the others had already guessed. (She had always been naive.) He was never going to leave her alone, not as long as he still thought she belonged to him. And as far as he was concerned, she would always be his.

Ninka held him like a doll, crooning to him in the language of her childhood, the one she used with Afrit. Efa thought of Idain, dismembered in the water. It had been so excessive for his crimes. It wouldn't be enough for Paul. She wasn't afraid anymore, she wasn't angry (there would be time for rage), she just needed him gone. There was already blood in the water.

Her teeth tore through his clothes and into his gut more easily than she had expected. It was foul, pieces of him in her mouth and in the water, but she was too practical a girl, and too long a hunter, to let that deter her. He screamed and beat at her and Ninka held him like a child until there was nothing left to hold.

{ 8 }

WHEN IT WAS OVER, BEFORE SHE'D HAD A CHANCE TO GET HER BREATH, SHE THOUGHT, NINKA ISN'T THE SORT OF PERSON I SHOULD BE AROUND. Look at what she just did. Undoubtedly what she had done was worse. She wondered when she would start to regret it.

Bettan was retching over the side of the boat when Efa got there. Efa shed her sealskin and scrambled in to rub her back. Her hair, still dripping, was already pinned out of the way. (The only time, Efa thought uncharitably, that adopting human customs had ever done anyone any good.) Louise had thrown a thick woolen blanket over her shoulders.

"Hush," Efa said, an arm around Bettan. "You're okay."

Eventually she stopped puking and wiped her mouth on her hand. Ninka and Afrit were not generally squeamish, but Efa noticed that they had stationed themselves on the opposite side of the boat from the vomit and gore.

"Is he dead?" Bettan asked once she'd turned around to face the others. The temperature was dropping, and she was covered in goosebumps.

Efa carefully closed her mouth and looked down to the water, which was soupy with... pieces. "Yeah," she said. "He's gone."

"You can say that," Louise said. "His own mother wouldn't recognize him now."

She had the decency to look embarrassed when Bettan burst into tears.

Efa put a hand on either side of Bettan and leaned in towards her, the tops of their foreheads touching. She babbled, offering reassurances that Bettan refused to take. "It's okay, it's okay," she said. "What's wrong? You're safe now."

Bettan's nose was dripping. "I have to go and talk to my grandmother," she said. "If we go now, we can be there and back before dark."

"You already said goodbye."

She sat up, her back straight, the blanket around her open in the front. She looked a mess, bits of snot and worse over her face, but she was also dead serious. "That was before I realized I was going to kill my husband."

"You didn't kill him, I-" But then she realized that was probably not the way to go.

"And someone needs to look after the house. The goats will need to be milked." She looked like she was counting off the chores that still needed to be done. She tugged the blanket so that it covered her chest. "Take me back."

For a moment, nobody said anything. Then Afrit pulled herself up beside them and said, "Well, if that's what she wants-"

"Absolutely not," said Louise. "You can't expect this woman to be on our side."

"She loves me." Bettan sounded absolutely certain. Efa would not have stood against her.

But she wouldn't have stood against Louise, either. "I'll bet," she said, tone absolutely flat. "But she'll have you killed. That or she'll keep you from leaving, and this time we'll have to burn the whole town to get you back."

They would do it, Efa thought, if they had to.

But Bettan crumpled. "Take me wherever," she said. "What's the point? I can't even get my sealskin on."

"I can fix that," Efa said, reaching out to touch Bettan's dress where it had torn at the neck. They were on the beach an hour away from Bettan's house. It had been clear to everyone that Bettan - and, for that matter, Efa - needed to stop for the day, but Louise had insisted that they go at least that far.

Ninka, Afrit and Louise had a fire. She could hear the crackling and Ninka's keening laughter. But they had settled apart from the group and let Louise bring them food. They both wanted some space, and anyway Bettan was wary of the others.

"Really?" she said. "My clothes back home are probably gone by now."

Efa stretched out on the sand, her arms folded behind her head. "I think Rees is keeping them for us. But it's just a little tear, and you snapped some of the laces. I'll get to it as soon as we get home."

Bettan's hands were balled up in her sealskin. She hadn't let go of it for a moment, not even to eat. "I don't think I can go home. What are they going to think of me?"

"They love you. Everyone loves you."

"They thought I was a slut before I went off with some man," she said.

"You didn't-"

Efa was starting to hate the way Bettan sounded these days, both sad and certain. "That's how they'll see it. And now I can't even-" She cut herself off. "And I was going to get married some day."

"Do you even want that anymore?"

She thought it over. "I don't know. But I did, and I don't want to let this change me."

Efa wiggled closer, so that Bettan's knee was touching her side. "Do you get a choice? It didn't even happen to me and I feel like, I don't know."

Bettan nodded. "No, you're right. You're different now. I just don't remember what we were like before." She looked over at the fire and bit her lip. "Are you and that fishwife girl..."

Efa froze and closed her eyes. Ninka had a lot of qualities, but discretion wasn't one of them. It was easy to fake it among strangers, pretend that she was just going along with strange fishwife customs, but Bettan knew her. "Which one?" she said.

"The dark one with the pink tail."

"She's my friend."

Bettan's tone wasn't quite accusing. "She kissed you."

Only once, and she'd hoped that no one had seen, but it had been on the fingertips, like she was a lady. And there was no denying the way Ninka looked at her, like she was precious and might break. "I'm so sorry," Efa said. "I haven't told anybody. I didn't mean to-"

"Shhhh," Bettan said, and laid her hand flat on Efa's belly. "Baby, they're like something out of a story. Of course you'd fall in love with one."

She frowned. "You're the romantic one."

"You came all this way for me, and you think I'm the romantic." Bettan laughed. "Tell me what happened."

"I don't know. I always thought it'd be a boy. And then I met her, and it was like, wow, this is what Bettan's been talking about all this time."

Bettan's smile was wistful. "Do you really love her?"

"I think so," Efa said. "We haven't done anything, and I don't know if we will - I don't think sirens even get married. But I want to be with her. Are you mad?"

"No," she said.

"I know it's not normal."

"I don't care," Bettan said. "The only thing that matters is that you want it. And, you have to promise you won't leave me."

Efa sat up. "Never," she said. "Not for my whole life, no matter what happens."

Bettan put a hand on Efa's shoulder and pushed her back, smiling. "Don't. Some day you'll get married, and you'll want kids, and-"

"You'll still be my best friend."

"And I know more about this than you do, so listen to me." Efa didn't think that was fair. She couldn't help that she was the younger one. But she shut up anyway. "Eventually things'll change, and that's fine, I know that. But you have to wait until I'm better again."

Efa shook her head. "There's nothing wrong with you. You're free now. Something bad happened, that's all."

"I feel like there's something wrong with me," she said. "And my sealskin agrees."

"That's a problem," Efa admitted. "But it could be any number of things. Maybe you just need to remember how."

Bettan gave her a look.

"Okay, probably not. But it could be you were just too scared."

"Have you ever had trouble changing because you were too scared?"

"No." She sighed and leaned forward, her elbows on her knees. "But I also know I've never been more afraid than I was today."

"I have," she said quietly. She didn't make eye contact. "I'm just worried - what if he turned me human?"

"That's not even possible."

"You've met selkies who married humans before," she pointed out. "After a while you stop really being a seal. What if-"

"You're still you," Efa said. "This didn't change anything."

Bettan pursed her lips. "You have to stay with me until I'm sure."

"Do you eat with your hands or with your teeth?" Bettan asked, just barely treading water far from the shore. She had gotten hysterical again, Efa thought unnecessarily, and tossed her sealskin on the floor of the rowboat, swimming off like she might let the sea take her.

"Both," Afrit said. She had followed Bettan out, leaving Efa to sit and sulk. She dived almost like a heron, her tail so long that most of it was still visible high above the water, and came back with long fistfuls of mussels, prawns, a squirming alefish, silt pouring out from between her fingers and down her wrists. She laid back into the water and set her catch on the curve below her ribs, picked up a prawn. "Whatever's easiest."

On the rowboat, Louise looked over the horizon and huffed.

"I'm sorry," Efa whispered. She could hear Afrit cracking a mussel open and the soft slurp as Bettan swallowed it, and the noise reminded her to stay quiet.

"I want to help her," Louise said, although perhaps it had only been in theory. "But there's only one way to bring her home, and it goes much slower when we have to keep stopping so she can whine."

"I never used to eat in this body," Bettan said, and Efa could hear in her voice how strange it was to have fingers. "Except if there was bread, or while I was waiting to dance. But I guess now I'll have to."

Efa didn't know what to say, to Louise or to cover her guilt. She took her sealskin and Bettan's and held them together, jaw-to-nose and tail-to-tail, and folded them into a parcel in her lap. "That's not fair," she said. "She has a lot to be upset about."

"Not fair," Louise said, "is that I have to row both of you home with this sunburn."

But she must have known that she wasn't being reasonable, because she locked the oars and hunted through her bag, took out her small cast iron file and a piece of wood that was going to be a bowl. Efa took the sealskins, hers feeling warm and alive and Bettan's like it wasn't quite really there, and set them on the edge of the boat, rested her head on them and closed her eyes. It was impossible to relax, the sawing noises so alien and the shame so familiar. She didn't even smile when Ninka came around the other side of the boat and pulled her hair out, started braiding it like a rope.

She hated being the good one and she hated being the one whose suspicions were always right and she hated that she had done what she'd meant to, even when no one had thought she could, and that it had changed so little.

There was a thin jagged noise like a fingernail ripping. Efa looked up. Afrit was slicing the prawns down their backs with her claws. They were so translucent, squirming aimlessly as she tore open their shells, that they reminded Efa of blown glass. She was suddenly hungrier than she'd been in days, like maybe if she caught something fresh it would get the taste of blood out of her teeth.

And Bettan was hungry, too; Efa could see it in the way she watched the prawns helplessly unfurling, the way she sank in the water so that her eyes were big and open above the sea foam.

Afrit pulled the prawn apart and bit, its whole body sliding out of its shell. "You have to start in the middle," she said. "And not get intimidated." She handed Bettan another one.

Bettan took it so seriously, looked it over, rinsed the silt from the undercarriage. "This is as big as my husband's arms," she murmured, and broke off its head.

They stopped off at the Hungry Hogfish as soon as they got home. Bettan, who had spent months apart from the sea, didn't want to have to look at it or smell its crisp air. Ninka and Afrit said - and Efa counted every single one of her blessings twice, a dozen times - that they understood, that they would wait until Bettan wanted to come back to the water. So they walked into town, Efa and Louise flanking Bettan, though she stood tall and shook off their touches when they tried to guide her.

Nellie and Jesse sat at the furthest back table in the Hogfish. They were on the same bench, his arm around her waist, her eyes closed. But the chill breeze hit her, perhaps: she opened her eyes and looked over at Bettan, Efa and Louise.

She stood and came to them quickly, picking her way through the packed hall as only an innkeeper's daughter could. She kissed Louise's cheek and said, "I'll get my father." Then she ran to the back.

Jesse came up after her; he bowed to Bettan and introduced himself.

"Beth," she started to say, and then corrected herself. "Bettan." She smiled, glanced over at Louise. Efa couldn't tell if she seemed particularly unhappy or if it was just the way she carried her sorrow. "But you know that. Were you part of the, uh, rescue party?"

"I helped in every way I could," he said, and gave a self-deprecating shrug. Efa found him perfectly charming, and he was certainly handsome. Bettan liked men who weren't too cocky, who were conscious of her status as a lady and intended to treat her right. (She also liked men who didn't much care about anything but that she wore a skirt. She liked men.) But she didn't seem to notice him.

George came out from the back, Nellie following. Efa had been worried that taking Bettan to the Hogfish would be a bad idea - that she would crumple under the pressure of being in a crowd, though perhaps the worst of it had happened in private - and when she saw Bettan's face, all her fears were realized. Bettan was frozen, one arm wrapped around her tiny waist and the other fist shoved in her mouth.

George stopped up short a few feet from them. "Darlin," he said, or maybe something else, it was so quiet. And then, hesitating just a moment, he took Bettan into his arms.

There was time for Efa to start to feel dizzy from holding her breath, for Louise to get a look on her face like she was about to tell him to back off, and then Bettan unravelled and clung to him.

"It's all right," he said. "I've got you."

Nellie looked away; Jesse looked to her. Efa and Louise didn't let up for a second.

"I need a place to stay," Bettan said. "I can't go back to them."

"Anything," he said. She stepped back and blinked her eyelashes dry. "I've got a room upstairs."

He headed in that direction. Without discussing it, Efa and Bettan followed him, and the rest stayed behind.

The upstairs of the Hungry Hogfish consisted of a few rooms off a long hallway. Efa had never been up there before, though she suspected (it wasn't the sort of thing a respectable girl would ever admit to) that Bettan had sometimes visited men in their rooms. George led them to the room at the end of the hall and unlocked it. Then he handed the key to Bettan.

"That's the only copy," he said, "so please don't lose it."

"Thank you," she said.

They stood there. Efa put an arm around Bettan. George said, "Would you like to talk?"

"She just-"

"Hush," Bettan interrupted her. And then, very graciously, like the wife of a general or a duke, "Come on in."

The room held a small dresser and a bed large enough to fit two, if they were friendly. George got the lamps lit and the girls sat on the bed.

"She's had a very difficult time of it," Efa said. "You have to-"

Bettan very nearly growled. "Efa."

"It's fine," he said. "I just want to know that you're okay."

"I am," Bettan said. But she seemed to reconsider. "My husband's dead, anyway."

"I can't imagine," he said.

"It was, surprisingly, not the worst thing that's ever happened to me." She laughed. "Though I'm not sure what was."

She looked so fragile all the time, or maybe it was just the finery she wore, the gloss of her hair, the way her lips kept trembling. Maybe it was just that it had been a while. None of them were sure what to say.

George broke the silence. "I don't think it was right," he said. "What happened to you. I don't know how they got you back, and I don't know what happened to that man. But I'm glad."

"Me, too." Bettan clasped her hands and stared at them. "I just don't understand..." She turned to Efa. "You should go check on the others. I'm sure they already know every awful detail of what happened, but you can preserve a little of my privacy."

"Louise wouldn't-"

"Louise," Bettan said, "is exactly what I'm worried about."

The two hadn't gotten along beyond what manners required. Neither, as far as Efa could tell, considered the other to be the right sort of woman. "Are you sure you're going to be okay with being alone? After...?"

The look Bettan gave her was scathing, and she spoke through her teeth. "You don't need to worry that I'll forget if you don't remind me." But she couldn't stay mad for long. She sighed, and she pressed her head against Efa's shoulder. "If something awful happened to you," she whispered, "you'd run to your father straightaway."

And it was true, so she left.

Rees found them a few days later on the island where Efa had been hiding the fishwives. "Efa," he called, coming up over the crest of the beach. Then, he saw them both and - this had been happening for years, Efa knew it was coming - his attention shifted fully to Bettan. "You're home."

Bettan shifted, her arms wrapping around her body. Louise had gone to the selkie village for them and gotten their things, so she was back in her own clothes. She stood and let Rees come to her. Efa sat by the fire, roasting some fish that the fishwives had caught for them. Ninka and Afrit were seeing to their own dinner, which was good. They didn't much know or care for Rees.

"Was she right?" he said, not too loud, when he got to Bettan. "Did you really...?"

"Yes," Bettan said.

He gathered her in his arms, her head tucked under his chin. Efa closed her eyes and felt the warmth of the fire, the smoke weaving around her.

"Was it okay?" Rees asked. "You must be so different. How long before you have to go back?"

Bettan started laughing and stepped away. "You don't understand." But she said it like she was talking about something completely trivial, like he'd guessed her favorite color wrong. "Efa killed him. I'm free."

Rees turned to her. "You what?"

Efa stood, but Bettan got there first. "Don't get mad," she said. "He was my husband, I get to decide if it was the right thing to do."

He frowned. "Murder is never-"

She put her hands on his sides and stood on her tiptoes to kiss his cheek, and he relented. "Sit down," she said. "Efa's making dinner, and there's more to tell."

They sat around the fire, Rees and Efa on either side of Bettan. "How did you do it?" he said.

Efa felt sick thinking about it. "I just sort of, with my teeth."

That took him a second. Then he said, "You can't tell anyone. They - Efa, humans kill each other over things like that. If they find out, you'll be hanged."

"But I'm a selkie," she said. She hadn't considered consequences, just what she needed to do to make him stop.

"Because humans are so nice to us." He dug both of his hands into his hair and tugged. "I can't believe you. Don't we have enough problems getting along without you going around killing them?"

"Stop," Bettan said. "They don't need to find out. Unless you're going to tattle?"

"She's my sister," he said. "My stupid, stubborn, murderous sister."

Efa sighed in relief. "Thank you," she whispered.

He reached behind Bettan and touched Efa's back. "At least now things can go back to how they were."

Efa and Bettan made eye contact, and then Efa grabbed a stick and poked at the fire.

The silence stretched. Bettan said, "I can't change anymore."

He leaned forward to get a better look at them. He wasn't the sort to sit still for anything. "Where's your sealskin?" he said. "What happened to it?"

"Nothing," she said, but she crawled over the few steps necessary to retrieve it for him.

It pooled in his lap, and he examined it methodically, the way that Efa would have gone over a length of cloth. "It's fine," he said at length. "And it's still wet." When sealskins died - usually along with the person who wore them - they dried and cracked, like badly maintained leather.

"I don't know why," Bettan said.

Rees nodded slowly. "You didn't..."

"What?"

He made a face and swallowed. "Lay with him."

She grabbed her sealskin back. "How come I can't win with you? You think I should have stayed, but you still get to be squeamish about what I had to do."

"I don't think you should have stayed."

"You don't think I should have stopped him," Efa said.

At the same time, Bettan said, "You didn't come for me."

"I'm sorry," he said. "I just mean, it could be that."

Bettan put her elbows on her knees and held her face in her hands, her hair falling into her eyes. "Would that do it?" she asked.

"If the baby's human, yeah. You can't change unless he can change with you." He shrugged. "I figured you'd know that, being girls."

"We don't spend a lot of time with humans," Efa said. She felt numb. She pulled the fish away from the fire and set it to the side to cool. "She can't really be pregnant. She seems fine."

"She's hardy," Rees said. "You probably won't even be able to tell until she starts to show."

"Great," Bettan said. She hadn't looked up. "Couldn't it be something else?"

"If it is, it's nothing I've ever heard of before," he said.

Efa put on her most sympathetic smile. "It'll be okay," she said. "Come eat and tell me what you're going to do."

Bettan sat up a little and brushed her hair out of her face. She took the fish and broke it into pieces. If it were up to Efa, they'd be eating it fresh-caught and raw, but their human bodies only tolerated that for so long. "I don't know," she said. "I just found out."

"Marry me," Rees said.

"What?" Bettan said, her mouth full.

"You can't raise a child by yourself."

"Try and stop her," Efa said. "Besides, she won't be alone. She's got me."

He rolled his eyes. "I'm not going to let this ruin your life," he said to Bettan. "I love you too much for that."

"Like a sister," Efa clarified.

"Not really."

"Stop," Bettan said. She looked drawn. "I don't want to get married."

Rees stopped. "I didn't mean - of course you wouldn't. We don't have to do anything. I won't even touch you. Whatever you need."

She stared at him, her jaw tight, for a moment. "That's not what I want, either."

"I would be good to you," he said.

"Yeah," she said to him. "I know you would."

Ninka swam to the surface, and Efa followed her up. When she was a seal, Efa still read Ninka as more of a predator than a friend, but swimming with her was one of her favorite things.

"So," Ninka said. "I was wondering?"

"What?" Efa said.

Ninka frowned. She was beginning to understand the rudiments of Sealish, but it came slowly to her. Meaning in Sealish was defined more by different tones and contexts than by particular words, and, to Efa's surprise, Ninka was more attuned to higher-pitched noises than rough barks. (That shouldn't have been a surprise, with all the wailing and whistling and screeching she did.) "Wondering," she repeated herself.

Efa slipped out of her sealskin.

Ninka was visibly relieved. "What did your brother say?"

She had been free of that discussion for less than an hour, and only because Rees and Bettan had pushed her away and told her to leave them to themselves. Efa groaned and put her head down on Ninka's shoulder, the water rising up to touch her face. "Bettan's going to have a baby."

"Is she very upset?"

"What do you mean?" She held her sealskin in one hand and put the other arm around Ninka's waist. "A child is always a good thing."

Ninka's tail swished around them; Efa could feel the water moving under the waves. "Does your friend think so?"

Probably. "She'll come around," Efa said. "It's a shock."

"Mmm." She wasn't listening. She pressed her lips to the space above Efa's ear and whispered, "You're free now, too."

"This isn't about me. It's always been about getting Bettan safe."

"But you couldn't do anything until you'd found her. Now you can do whatever you want." She paused, and Efa could feel her swallow. "We can be together."

Efa picked her head up and examined Ninka's face. They were so close it was hard to see everything. Ninka's mouth was open, waiting, and she didn't look away. Efa kissed her, once, twice, until she closed her eyes. "We are together," she said. "We've been together."

Ninka's teeth showed. "Somewhere that isn't awful," she complained. "It's cold here, and someone could take you next."

"Everyone I know is here," Efa said.

That didn't mean anything to Ninka except what it meant to Efa. "We could be somewhere warm. There wouldn't have to be anyone but us."

Efa let the waves carry her a bit away. She wrapped her sealskin around her shoulders. "I'm not leaving Bettan," she said.

Ninka pursed her lips, and for a moment she was more girl than monster. "Oh," she said. And then, quickly, "I knew you weren't forever. I didn't mean-"

"Hush," Efa said. "What I'm saying is, she's the most important thing in my life right now. And I don't know how long that'll be. I need you to know that and decide you'll stay anyway."

Ninka was quiet for a while. Efa looked into the water to give her space. "I won't be your wife," she said. "I'm a siren."

Efa nodded, and then shook her head. "I think you can be both," she said, unsure. "I think - you left everything to be with me. And that's enough. All I need you to be is here."

Acknowledgments

I can't hope to thank all of the people who made it possible for me to write this book.

I was blessed with the best family that anyone could hope for. For encouraging me to explore the world and always giving me a place to return home, for telling me your stories and asking me to write mine down, for pretending to like Avril Lavigne so I would feel confident in myself, for bringing me to Take Back the Night and buying me shirts at Pride, thank you. I owe a special debt to my mother, who shepherded me through the most painful times in my life with such grace that it was easy to forget that she was learning, too.

To XYN and the Funk family, I love each of you and I am so proud of us. Can you believe how far we've made it?

My fiancée, Bridget, is the love of my life and the best decision I have ever made. I am so grateful to be marrying a woman who is not only willing to tolerate that I write, but considers it a major part of our life together. I love you because of everything.

And finally, a hearty thanks to Mary Dykeman, who was right when she said "The hardest part is going to be how long it will take for things to get better," and gave me a Laura Nyro album.

ABOUT THE AUTHOR

Tori Curtis is a gay woman with an office job who views family, disability, and identity through classic speculative fiction tropes. She lives in upstate New York with her steadfast fiancée and fewer dogs than said fiancée would like. Eelgrass is her first novel.

Follow me online!
toricurtiswrites.com
@tcurtfish